When Mak put his hand on the small of her back to guide her through the throng, Neena ceased to think at all. *Couldn't* think!

So she danced with Mak beneath the stars—with a stranger to whom she was attracted—a stranger that the few brain cells still operating in her head warned her to avoid.

At all costs!

And then Mak touched her baby bump— very gently at first, then settling his hand on it. When he murmured, 'Next year you'll have someone special with whom to share your Christmas,' Neena felt a wave of sadness sweep over her. Yes, it would be good to have a baby in the house for Christmas. But right now the two of them as a family seemed a little meagre...

Meredith Webber says of herself, 'Some ten years ago, I read an article which suggested that Mills and Boon were looking for new medical authors. I had one of those "I can do that" moments, and gave it a try. What began as a challenge has become an obsession— though I do temper the "butt on seat" career of writing with dirty but healthy outdoor pursuits, fossicking through the Australian Outback in search of gold or opals. Having had some success in all of these endeavours, I now consider I've found the perfect lifestyle.'

Recent titles by the same author:

THE HEART SURGEON'S BABY SURPRISE**
THE HEART SURGEON'S SECRET CHILD**
CHILDREN'S DOCTOR, MEANT-TO-BE WIFE*
THE SHEIKH SURGEON'S BABY†

**Jimmie's Children's Unit*
Crocodile Creek
†Desert Doctors*

GREEK DOCTOR: ONE MAGICAL CHRISTMAS

BY
MEREDITH WEBBER

⊛™ MILLS & BOON®

First published in Great Britain 2009
Large Print edition 2010
Harlequin Mills & Boon Limited,
Eton House, 18-24 Paradise Road,
Richmond, Surrey TW9 1SR

© Meredith Webber 2009

ISBN: 978 0 263 21084 2

Harlequin Mills & Boon policy is to use papers that are
natural, renewable and recyclable products and made
from wood grown in sustainable forests. The logging and
manufacturing process conform to the legal environmental
regulations of the country of origin.

Printed and bound in Great Britain
by CPI Antony Rowe, Chippenham, Wiltshire

GREEK DOCTOR: ONE MAGICAL CHRISTMAS

PROLOGUE

'So I don't know what to do!'

Mak stared at his only sister in disbelief.

Never in his life had he heard this strong-willed, determined, driven woman admit such a thing.

'Have you talked to her?'

Helen shook her head.

'I've written, I've sent emails, and heard nothing in reply. I can hardly just go out there and land on her doorstep. What if she shut the door in my face? Besides, it's impossible for me to get away. Since Dad's death I've been running the business and trying to keep Mum going—you know how she is—the two deaths coming so close together, it's as if she's given up living. Look at Christmas—her Christmas productions rivalled the Oscar presentations. Feast and family, that was her mantra. This year she's doing nothing and when I suggested I do it, she just shrugged.'

Mak was still puzzled. Yes, Helen was busy and, yes, his mother did seem to have under-standably lost her zest for life, but did that add up to so much consternation? Wouldn't time—?

'There's also the cousins,' Helen muttered.

Ah!

He waited for Helen to explain, knowing she would, eventually.

It came with a sigh.

'The cousins are doing their best to take control of the business and if we lose control of Hellenic, Mum will have to watch all Dad built up go into other hands. She'll feel as if his whole life was for nothing.'

While Helen paced the office at the top of Hellenic Enterprises city headquarters, Mak con-sidered what he'd just learned. With his father's blessing, he'd gone into medicine rather than following the parental footsteps into engineer-ing, but as well as Helen, half a dozen of his cousins, children of his father's sisters, had entered the family firm.

And held shares in it!

He frowned, realising that, although still part of the company, he knew less and less of what went on within it these days, his studies and work leaving him little time to read the company reports. And his father's unexpected death had left him with a lot of problems to sort out, as he was the executor of his father's personal estate.

'*Can* they take over? I mean, do they have the power to do that—the majority of shares between them? And what would it mean if they did?'

'They can if they get that woman to vote with them in the extraordinary general meeting they've called for January, and the way they are talking they already have her vote in the bag.'

'You know this for certain?' Mak asked, aware of the bias Helen felt against 'that woman'.

'I'm pretty sure and equally sure money has changed hands. Con was out there just last week, ostensibly to check on the experimental power plant but he's never been interested in geo-thermal power before.' Helen hesitated before adding, 'And there was a rather large item in his expenses, listed as a donation.'

Mak felt himself frowning.

'Did you ask him about it?'

'How could I?' Helen muttered. 'I shouldn't

have seen the information—not until the next board meeting when we all table our expenses.'

'You were spying on him?' Mak couldn't hide his disbelief.

'I was not—it was just that Marge, Dad's old secretary, alerted me to it as she typed up the agenda.'

Which was the same as spying, Mak considered, but that wasn't the issue right now.

'Maybe Con really was checking on the power plant, and the donation was just that. After all, he'd hardly bribe the woman with the firm's money.'

'Well, he wouldn't use his own,' Helen snapped. 'You don't know Con like I do—he's changed since he married for the third time. I reckon his wife keeps her hands on the purse strings. He's as tight as a—as a you know what.'

Mak considered his easygoing cousin and wondered if the third wife might not be on to something—keeping control of Con's spending. Was she also behind the push to take over the company? It didn't seem like something Con, or any of the cousins, would instigate…

'This is all supposition, Helen. Let's give Con the benefit of the doubt for the moment. And in any case, why are you worried about a takeover?

You'd still be part of the company, probably still CEO, as I can't see any of them wanting that job.'

'I wouldn't stay,' Helen said, her face pale and her lips tight. 'I know how they think and the way they see the future. Heaven knows, we've argued it often enough in board meetings. If they take over it will be the end of Dad's dream to produce clean power, for one thing. They see that as someone else's job or something for the future. Anything experimental is expensive, and there's no certainty of a return. The cousins want profits that are guaranteed and they want them now which would mean taking the firm in a different direction, looking more towards structural engineering than Dad ever did, and probably merging with a bigger firm.'

Mak understood what she was saying but his mind had snagged on the earlier conversation—at the thought of money changing hands, and Con's third wife, and manipulative women in general. The juxtaposition had prodded another thought in his mind—a very unwelcome one.

Theo had been shameless in his pursuit of women, casually promiscuous, but he had always been careful, assuring Mak that he always took precautions—that he wasn't totally irresponsible.

So had this pregnancy been planned—not by Theo but by the woman in question? Had she seen an opportunity to either trap Theo into marriage, or to benefit in some other way?

She'd benefit all right if the cousins gave—or had already given—her money for her votes, benefit at the expense of Helen and his mother, at the expense of his father's dreams and at the expense of their small family unit, which had always been so tight.

Mak felt anger stir at the thought of a deliberate pregnancy, having been caught up in similar circumstances himself, years ago. Although no one, he was sure, could be as devious as Rosalie had been! However, to be fair, the 'money changing hands' scenario was only supposition on Helen's part. As far as he knew, this woman hadn't made any move to ingratiate herself with the family—in fact, the opposite was true, which brought another problem in its train. Mak's Greek genetic heritage was strongly aligned to family values—family made you what you were, and children needed family.

She had a name, of course, the woman, but it was never mentioned in the family—particularly not in Helen's hearing. Any more than Theo's reputation as a ladies' man was discussed in Helen's hearing. To his sister, her only child had been perfect in every way—handsome, clever, loyal, a loving son and an obedient grandson, following the family tradition by studying engineering—the designated successor to his grandfather, the designated heir to the massive conglomerate of businesses that made up Hellenic Enterprises.

But Theo was dead, killed in a motor vehicle accident that had also taken the lives of three of his friends. Four young people tragically dead because of speed and alcohol, and Mak, who as a top emergency room doctor saw far too many young lives wasted this way, had felt more fury than grief when first he'd heard the news. Grief for his nephew, and his sister's suffering, had come, but the fury had returned when Mak had learned that Theo had been irresponsible enough to leave behind an unborn child.

A child who would be family…

'What stage are you at with the exploration

teams out there?' he asked Helen, as an idea that filled him with horror started to form, unwanted, in his head.

'We've found hot rocks close to the surface and although the exploration teams will remain out there, we've sent more men in to build the experimental power plant. Now it's nothing more than pipes and pumps but once we're satisfied that the rocks are suitable for our needs, we'll go ahead with a proper set-up.'

'So, you've the first crews, and more men for the power plant and the likelihood that even more men will be going out there shortly. And if a power plant goes ahead, some of those men will be there permanently so families would be joining them. I'd think you must be putting pressure on a lot of the town's resources but in particular the medical services if there's only one doctor in town.'

Helen nodded, but it was a vague reaction, and Mak could almost see the cloud of grief that still enveloped her.

'Helen?' he prompted, but gently this time.

She nodded again.

'We are,' she said, visibly pulling herself

together. 'In fact, Theo suggested the company fund another medical practitioner, if only for the duration of the exploration, but he might have had an ulterior motive—that woman might have been prompting him. The company could certainly afford it but how do we find out if that's what the town really needs?'

Mak knew how they could find out because there was already a raging argument going on his head. Go out and check on things for himself? No way, he was on study leave, it was midsummer, the temperature would be up in the stratosphere, he had his thesis to complete. On the other hand, the family was important to him and right now it appeared to be falling apart. Helen, on whom he had always relied to keep things running smoothly, was struggling—physically as well as emotionally, he suspected. His mother—well, if ever anyone needed some new interest in her life, it was her and surely a great-grandchild could supply that interest…

He'd have to think about it.

There was no time to think about it.

'I don't know what to do,' Helen said, taking the conversation back to where it had started, but now her voice was a feathery whisper, filled with pain and loss. 'I've lost my son and now I'll never know my grandchild.'

'I'll sort it out,' he heard himself say. 'I'll go tomorrow and that will give me the whole weekend to sort out somewhere to stay and introduce myself to Dr Singh.'

CHAPTER ONE

HEADLIGHTS coming up the drive lit up the room, rousing Neena from the comfortable doze she was enjoying in front of the television. Not a patient— at this time of the night, getting on for midnight, patients would go straight to the hospital.

Unless there was an emergency out at the exploration site! No, they'd have phoned her, not driven in.

She eased herself off the couch, aware these days of the subtle redistribution of her body weight. Tugging her T-shirt down to hide the neat bump of Baby Singh, she made her way to the front door, opening it in time to see a tall, dark-haired man taking the steps two at a time, coming closer and closer to her, looming larger and larger.

A tall, dark-haired stranger.

'Can I help you?' she asked, checking him out

automatically in the light shed by the motion sensors above the door. No visible blood, no limp, no favouring of one or other limb, and gorgeous, just gorgeous—tall, black-haired, chiselled features…

Chiselled features?

Had pregnancy finally turned her brain to mush?

And he hadn't answered her enquiry. He'd simply reached the top of the steps and stopped, his dark gaze, eyes too shadowed to reveal colour, seemingly fastened on her face.

She was beautiful!

Mak had no idea why this should come as such a surprise to him. After all, Theo had hardly been noted for bedding women who weren't. Had he, Mak, been thinking maybe Theo had been desperate, out here in the middle of nowhere, and settled for someone available rather than stunning? Was that why he was standing here like a great lummox, staring at the straight, slim figure in shorts and T-shirt—staring at a face of almost luminous beauty?

Except that her left cheek was reddened down one side, as if she'd been sleeping against something hard.

Maybe it was the heat, pressing against him like a warm blanket, that was affecting his brain.

'Are you ill? Injured?'

Her voice was soft, and concerned, not about the arrival of a stranger on her doorstep at getting on to midnight but about the state of his health.

'No, but you *are* Dr Singh?'

'Yes, and you are?'

He had to get past his surprise at seeing her—had to stop staring at clear olive skin and sloe-shaped dark eyes, framed by lashes long enough to seem false; at a neat pointed chin below lips as red as dark rose petals, the velvety red-black roses his mother grew.

'Mak Stavrou!' Right, he was back in control again, and had managed to remember his name, but she was still looking puzzled.

'Mak Stavrou,' she repeated, and it was as if no one had ever said his name before, so softly did the syllables fall from her lips.

She was a witch. She had to be. Witches had long black hair that gleamed blue in the veranda light. Witches would be able to handle this heat without showing the slightest sign of wilting.

He wiped sweat off his own brow and felt the dampness of it in his hair.

'The company doctor—you must have received an email.'

The still functioning part of his brain managed to produce this piece of information, while the straying neurones were still looking around for a black cat or a broomstick parked haphazardly in the corner of the veranda.

'Company doctor?' she said, shaking her head in a puzzled manner so the long strands of hair that he now saw had escaped from a plait that hung, schoolgirl fashion, down her back, swayed around her face.

'Check your emails—there'll be something there.'

'Check your emails?' she repeated, the red lips widening into a smile. 'Out here we have to take into account the vagaries of the internet, which seem to deem that at least one day in four nothing works. The big mistake most people, me included, made was thinking wireless would be more reliable than dial-up. At least with dial-up we all had phone lines we could use.'

Neena paused then added, 'Are you really a doctor?'

It was an absurd conversation to be having with a stranger in the middle of the night, and totally inhospitable to have left him standing on her top step, but there was something about the man—his size maybe?—that intimidated her, and she had the weirdest feeling that the best thing she could do was to send him away.

Far away!

Immediately!

'And what company? Oh, dear, excuse me. The exploratory drilling company, of course. They're staying on. I'd heard that. And they've sent a doctor?'

It still didn't make a lot of sense and she knew she was probably frowning at the man. She tried again.

'But shouldn't you be reporting to the site office—not that it would be open at this hour. Who sent you here?'

He shrugged impossibly broad shoulders and pushed damp twists of black hair off his forehead.

'*Nothing* is open at this hour. Believe me, I've tried to find somewhere. A motel, a pub, a garage—even the police station has a sign on the door telling people what number to phone in an emergency. And it's not as if it's that late—I mean, it's after eleven, but for the pub to be shut on a Friday night! Finally an old man walking a dog told me this was the doctor's house and I should try here.'

'It's the rock eisteddfod,' Neena explained, then realised from the look of blank incomprehension on his face that it wasn't an explanation he understood.

'The Australia-wide high-school competition—singing and dancing. Our high school was in the final in Sydney last week. In fact, they came second, and as most of the parents and supporters weren't able to travel to Sydney for the final, the school decided to put it on again here—but of course Wymaralong is too small to have a big enough hall, so it's on tonight down the road in Baranock.'

Disbelief spread across the man's face.

'Baranock's two hundred kilometres away—hardly down the road.'

She had to smile.

'Two hundred kilometres is nothing. Some of

the families with kids in the performance live another hundred kilometres out of town so it's a six hundred kilometre round trip, but they're willing to do it to encourage their children to participate in things like this.'

'*You're* not there!' Mak pointed out, totally unnecessarily, but the smile had disturbed something in his gut, making him feel distinctly uncomfortable. Or maybe it was the heat. He hoped it was the heat.

Whatever it was, his comment served to make her smile more widely, lending her face a radiance that shone even in the dim lighting of the front veranda.

'Someone had to mind the shop and take in stray doctors. So, if you can show me some identification, I *will* take you in, and tomorrow we can sort out somewhere for you to stay.'

'Did I hear you say you're taking in a stranger?'

A rasping voice from just inside the darkened doorway of the old house made Mak look up from the task of riffling through his wallet in search of some ID.

'Haven't you learnt your lesson, girl?'

The girl in question had turned towards the

doorway, where a small, nuggety man was now visible.

'I knew you were here to protect me, Ned,' she said. 'Come out and meet the new doctor.'

'New doctors let people know they're coming and they don't arrive in the middle of the night,' the small man said, moving out of the doorway so Mak could see him in the light on the veranda. A tanned, bald head, facial skin as wrinkled as a walnut, pale blue eyes fanned with deep lines from squinting into the sun, now studying Mak with deep suspicion.

'I've explained to Dr Singh there should have been an email, and I wasted an hour trying to find some accommodation in town. Here, my hospital ID from St Christopher's in Brisbane— I'm on study leave at the moment—and my driver's licence, medical registration card and somewhere in my luggage, a letter from Hellenic Enterprises, outlining my contract with them.'

The woman reached out a slim hand to take the offered IDs, but it was Ned who asked the question.

'Which is?'

A demand, aggressive enough for Mak, exhausted after an eleven-hour drive made even more tortuous by having to change a flat tyre, to snap.

'None of your business, but if you must know, I was about to explain to Dr Singh that the company has asked me to work with her to evaluate the needs of the community as far as medical practitioners and support staff are concerned. The company realises having their crews and now some families of the crews here is putting an extra strain on the town's medical resources and the powers that be at Hellenic are willing to fund another doctor and possibly another trained nursing sister, should that be advisable.'

'Realising it a bit late,' Ned growled. 'Those lads have been out there a full year.'

'But more are coming, Ned, and we *will* need to expand the medical service.' The woman spoke gently but firmly to the old man then turned to Mak. 'We're hardly showing you the famed country hospitality, putting you through the third degree out here on the steps. Come inside. You're right about there being no one in town tonight, but even if there had been, there are no rooms to be had at the pub or in either of the motels.'

She paused and grinned at him. 'Kind of significant, isn't it—coming on to Christmas and no room at the inn? But in Wymaralong it's been like that all year. The crews from the exploration teams and the travellers that service the machinery have taken every spare bed in town. You can stay here tonight, and tomorrow Ned can phone around to see if someone would be willing to take you in as a boarder.'

'Which you are obviously not,' Mak said, following her across the veranda and into a wide and blessedly cool hallway, rooms opening off it on both sides.

She turned, and fine dark eyebrows rose while the skin on her forehead wrinkled into a tiny frown.

'Obviously not what?'

'Willing to take me in as a boarder.'

'No, she's not!' Ned snapped, following behind Mak, right on his heels, ready, no doubt, to brain him with an umbrella from the stand inside the door if he made a wrong move.

The woman's lips moved but if it was a smile, it was a wry one.

'You can have a bed for the night,' she repeated. 'Tomorrow we'll talk.'

Then she waved her hand to the left, ushering

Mak into a big living room, comfortably furnished with padded cane chairs, their upholstery faded but looking homely rather than shabby. Low book-shelves lined one wall, and an old upright piano stood in a corner, its top holding a clutter of framed photographs, while set in front of every chair was a solid footrest, as if the room had been furnished with comfort as its primary concern.

And the air in here, too, was cool, although Mak couldn't hear the hum of an air-conditioner.

'Have a seat,' his hostess offered. 'Have you eaten anything recently? Ned could make you toast, or an omelette, or there's some leftover meatloaf. Dr Stavrou might like that in a sandwich, Ned. And tea or coffee, or perhaps a cold drink.'

Mak looked from the woman to Ned, who was still watching Mak, like a guard dog that hadn't let down its guard for one instant.

'A cup of tea and some toast would be great and the meatloaf sounds inviting, but you don't have to wait on me. If you lead me to the kitchen and show me where things are, I could help myself.'

'Not in my kitchen, you can't. Not while I'm here,' Ned growled—guard dog again—before disappearing further down the hall.

Now her visitor was sitting in her living room, Neena stopped staring at him and recalled her manners.

'I'm Neena Singh,' she said, introducing herself as if there was nothing strange in this near-midnight meeting, although suspicion was now stirring in her tired brain. She recalled something the man had said earlier. 'If you're on study leave, why are you here? Surely you're not studying the problems of isolated medical practitioners.'

'No, but it's not that far off my course. I'm finishing a master's degree, and my area of interest is in improving the medical aid offered by the first response team in emergency situations. I imagine in emergency situations out here you're the first response—you and the ambos. In major situations the flying doctor comes in, but you'd be first response.'

She couldn't argue, thinking of the number of times she'd arrived at the scene of a motor vehicle or farm accident and wished for more hands, more skilled help, more equipment and even better skills herself. Anything to keep the victims alive until they could be properly stabilised and treated.

'Do you work in the emergency field?'

The stranger nodded.

'ER at St Christopher's.'

'And the company plan is what? For you to work with me to gauge the workload in town or will you work solely with the work crew out on the site?'

'Not much point in working out on site when I need to find out how the additional population—now the men are here permanently they'll have family joining them—affects the medical services of the town,' he said, looking up at her so she saw his eyes weren't the dark brown she'd expected but a greenish hazel—unusual eyes and in some way uncannily familiar.

Like Theo's?

Futile but familiar anger tightened her shoulder-blades, and the suspicion she'd felt earlier strengthened. She tried to shrug off the anger *and* the suspicion. The man's name was Greek, so maybe there was a part of Greece where people had dark hazel eyes…

He was still talking—explaining something—but she'd lost the thread of the conversation, wanting only to escape his presence—to get out

of the room and shake herself free of tormenting memories.

And to think rationally and clearly about the
implications of the man's arrival in town!

'I'm sorry,' she said. 'I should have offered
earlier. You might want to use the bathroom,
freshen up. It's across the passage, turn left then
first door on the right.'

Getting rid of him, if only for a short time,
would be nearly as good as escaping herself, but
he didn't move.

'Thanks, but I did avail myself of the facilities
at the service station. The rest rooms weren't
locked—they even had a shower in there, so I
took advantage of that as well.'

'Most outback service stations provide
showers—for the truckies,' Neena said, impart-
ing the information like a tour guide. If escaping
the man's presence wasn't possible, then
neutral—tour-guide—conversation was the next
best thing. Later she could think about personal
issues. 'This is sheep and cattle country and the
animals are trucked to market, plus, of course,
all our consumer goods have to be trucked in.'

'And products for the farmers—stuff like

fencing wire,' Mak offered helpfully, wondering why the woman was so ill at ease in her own home. Or did she know who he was? That he was family? Unlikely Theo would have mentioned him. 'I have an Uncle Mak who disapproves of me' was hardly the kind of conversation that would lure a woman into bed.

'Yes, it did sound pathetic, didn't it?' Neena said, a slight smile playing at the corners of her lips. 'But I'd lost track of the conversation. I was dozing in front of the TV when you arrived and my mind was still half-asleep. I gather you want to work with me, and as far as I'm concerned, that's fantastic because I can learn from you. You've no idea how often I wish I had more skills in first response stuff. Oh, I get by, but there are so many new ideas that it's hard to keep up.'

Mak wished they'd kept talking about trucking. Neena's honest admission that she hadn't been listening to his conversation, followed by such an enthusiastic acceptance of his presence made him feel tainted and uneasy—unclean, really, for all he'd showered. And when she'd smiled—well, almost smiled— his gut had tightened uncomfortably, but he was fairly sure he could put that aside as a normal reaction to such a beautiful woman. It was the deception bothering him the most, but he could hardly announce now that he was really here to suss her out.

'I've made you toasted sandwiches with the meatloaf.'

Ned marched in, bearing a tray which he set down on a small table beside Mak's chair. 'And there's a pot of tea, but don't you go thinking you can have a cup, Miss Neena. You're sleeping bad enough as it is. I'll make you a warm milk if you want something.'

Mak smiled as Neena hid a grimace.

'No, thank you, Ned. I drank some milk earlier, as you very well know, and how can I have a cup of tea when you've only put out one cup?'

'You'd drink it from the pot if you got desperate enough,' Ned muttered as he made his way out of the room, pausing in the doorway to add, 'I've put clean sheets on the bed in the back room.'

A quick frown flitted across Neena's smooth brow.

'Does the back room have rats and cockroaches or is it just as far away from your room as it can possibly be?' Mak asked, and won another smile from his hostess.

'It's certainly not the best spare room in the house,' she admitted. 'And Ned does get over-protective. But I don't *think* there are rats or cockroaches.'

'Even if there were, I doubt it would worry me,' Mak said. 'It's a long drive and I'm tired enough to sleep on a barbed-wire fence. In fact, if it's okay with you, I might take my tray through and have the snack there. That way we can both get to bed.'

She turned away but not before he saw a blush rise in her cheeks. Surely not because he'd mentioned both of them getting to bed—it was hardly suggestive, the way he'd said it…

'Through here,' she was saying, and, tray in hand, he followed her, noting the bathroom she'd talked about earlier on the right then another two doors before they reached the end of the passage and the back room.

'Oh, dear,' she murmured as she opened the door and looked in, then turned back and ran her gaze over him from head to toe. 'I'd forgotten about the bed in here. You'll never fit.'

And over her shoulder Mak saw what she

meant for Ned had put sheets onto a rather small—perhaps child size—single bed, and even from the doorway, Mak could feel the heat emanating from the room.

'I heard him say he'd sleep on a barbed-wire fence,' the gravelly voice reminded them, and looking through a French door on the other side of the room, Mak saw Ned standing on the veranda.

On guard?

'Well, he can't sleep here. Honestly, Ned, sometimes I wonder if your main aim in life is to frustrate me. Come this way,' Neena added to Mak. 'There's a double bed that should take your height, if you sleep crossways, in the next bedroom, and that bedroom has an air vent as well. I'll get some sheets.'

She opened another door.

'I'll have it made up by the time you get your gear out of the car, and as far as I'm concerned you're welcome to stay here. This *is* the doctor's house after all.'

She was doing it to get her own back on Ned, Mak realised that immediately. He also realised it would give him an ideal opportunity to really get to know her!

So why did he feel uneasy?

Because of the deceit? Or because on first impression this woman was nothing like the manipulative gold-digger he'd envisioned?

'You don't have to put me up.' It was a token protest, brought on by the uneasiness, but she waved it away.

'Of course I don't, but sometimes I get very tired of being bossed around by every single person in this town. Sometimes I'd like to be allowed to make my own decisions. Now, get your things—you know where the bathroom is. I'll put some fresh towels in there.'

She whirled away, opening a cupboard near the back room, pulling out sheets and towels.

'Leave the sheets on the bed, I'll make it up,' Mak told her, and she silenced him with a glare.

'Don't you start,' she warned, marching back down the hall, slipping past him into the bedroom.

Mak set the tray down and left her to it, wondering just why the town would be so protective of her. Okay, so it was hard to get doctors to serve in country towns and the further outback you went the harder it became, but...

Maybe it was her pregnancy.

The phone was ringing as he re-entered the house, silenced when Neena must have answered it. He heard her say, 'I'll be right there,' and the click of a receiver being returned to its cradle.

'Bed's made,' she said, passing him in the passage. 'Towels in the bathroom.'

And she kept walking.

Dumping his bag, Mak followed her.

'You're going out on a call,' he said as his long strides caught up.

She nodded but her pace didn't slacken as she crossed the veranda and ran lightly down the steps—running when being back out in the hot night air immediately sapped his energy.

'I'll come with you,' he said, determined to get used to whatever the climate threw at him. 'It's what I'm here for, to see how you work.'

'You've been driving all day and you're tired,' she said, opening the door of a big four-wheel-drive that stood just off the main circular driveway. Then she turned to look at him. 'But it's probably your kind of thing and I could certainly use some help. An accident at the drilling site. The ambulance was out of town but it's on its way.'

Mak didn't answer, instead striding around the

car and climbing in the passenger side, relieved to find she'd already started the engine and had the air-con roaring.

'Motor vehicle?' he asked, and as Neena reversed the car competently onto the drive, she shook her head.

'I don't know how much you know about it, but if you're employed by Hellenic Enterprises presumably you know they've gone past the initial exploratory drilling stage and are setting up an experimental geo-thermal power station. Basically they pump water down into the bowels of the earth onto shattered hot rocks, and the heat of the rocks turns the water to steam, which comes up through different pipes and is harnessed and used to make electricity.'

Her explanation had holes in it but as a basic description of a scientific process it wasn't too bad.

'And what's happened?'

'A seam on a pipe burst and steam escaped. Two men badly burned, others less seriously.'

'Steam burns—bad business,' Mak said, wishing he had the facilities of St Christopher's burns unit here.

'The flying doctor's on the way. We stabilise

them as best we can and they'll fly them to somewhere with a burns unit.'

'So, it's a first response situation,' he said, turning to look at her. She was studying the road ahead, concentrating on the thin strip of bitumen, so all he could see was a clean, perfect profile—high forehead, straight nose, the flare of lips, the delicately pointed chin.

'Exactly,' she said. 'Most of our emergencies are. We stabilise people and send them on—some, if they're locals, come back so we know about the eventual outcome but many of them, travellers passing through, are never seen again.'

'Most emergency medicine is like that—I rarely see anything of the patients I treat once they've left the ER. Rarely hear how they've fared, for that matter.'

'And does that bother you?'

She glanced his way and he sensed she was really interested in his reply, an interest that intrigued him.

'Why do you ask?'

She smiled.

'I suppose because I know most of my patients so well. The local ones are part of my life and

I'm part of theirs so we work together to get the best outcomes for them. I can't imagine a scenario where I don't know what happens next.'

The words rang true, and Mak wondered if a woman who could be so involved in her patients' lives could also be the manipulative female he suspected she was.

Of course she could be. All human beings were multi-faceted.

'I suppose part of the fascination of medicine is that it offers so many different opportunities in its practice,' he said, although the way she'd spoken made him wonder about what *had* happened to some of the patients he'd treated. Just a few who'd made a big impression on him, or those who had been tricky cases...

'Anyway, I'm glad you're here for this job,' she continued. 'You probably have far more experience with burns than I do.'

Her gratitude made his gut squirm and her frank admission about her capabilities didn't fit with the picture he'd built up in his mind. Served him right for pre-judging?

He turned his mind from the puzzle this beautiful woman presented to the task ahead of them.

'Were the pipes in an enclosed space?'

She glanced his way again.

'I haven't been out there for a couple of weeks so I don't know what's been going on, but originally all the piping was exposed—right out in the open.'

Another glance then her attention switched back to the road. 'You're thinking inhalation injuries? Even outside, if they were close to the pipe when the accident happened…'

She paused, frowning as she thought, then asked, 'Would obvious facial burns always be indicative of inhalation injuries?'

She had a quick mind, something he usually admired—and enjoyed—in a woman, but in this woman?

'Yes, it should give us an indication. If there are signs of facial involvement—maybe even if there aren't—we should intubate them. If there's internal tissue damage that causes swelling—'

'Intubating later might be impossible,' Neena finished for him, happy to be talking medicine, although distinctly unhappy about this man's sudden intrusion into her life.

Was he simply who he said he was—someone

sent by the company to assess the strain the additional population was putting on medical services? Or had Theo's mother, the coldly formal Helen Cassimatis of the emails and letters, sent him?

He was quiet now. Maybe, like her, he didn't want to get too far ahead of himself before he saw the patients.

She risked a glance at him, pleased he was looking out the window into the darkness through which they passed.

A very good-looking man, but...

Greek name, Greek company...

Not that Neena hadn't expected it. Theo's complaints about his stifling family, while probably exaggerated, had suggested nothing less, and she'd doubted Theo's mother wouldn't do something to follow up the outrageous offers she'd made!

First there'd been an offer of financial help, followed closely by the suggestion that Neena move to the city so she could have the best medical attention. Then a letter just to let Neena know 'the family' had accommodation she could have rent-free in Brisbane so she wouldn't have to work.

And all so 'the family' could get their hands on

Neena's child! The same 'family' that had produced Theo—charming, intelligent, handsome and smart, and so cosseted and spoiled, so used to getting his own way, he'd taken Neena's panicky, and admittedly last-minute no as a tease and had forced her.

The squelchy feeling in her stomach wasn't as bad as it used to be, but she still couldn't think of that night without feeling a slight nausea. She breathed deeply, in and out, and concentrated on the road ahead.

They'd left the silent, deserted town well behind them and she pushed the memories equally far away.

The road was dead straight, a single-lane strip of bitumen that in daylight stretched to the horizon. Now, at night, a cluster of lights marked the site of the geo-thermal experimental station.

'Is there an airstrip at the site?' Mak asked. 'Can the flying doctors land there?'

Neena shook her head.

'At first it was just a couple of exploratory crews out here, drilling down to work out how far they needed to go to get to the hot rocks.

When they found them closer to the surface than they'd expected…'

She stopped and turned briefly towards him.

'I suppose you know the rocks can be anything from two to ten kilometres beneath the surface of the earth and apparently when you're drilling and pumping water and steam every metre makes a difference?'

'I know a bit about the process—I'm interested in all alternate power sources and geothermal in Australia makes a lot of sense. But you're saying that for exploratory purposes there was no need for an airstrip? Because the crews moved around?'

She nodded and Mak saw the frown he'd glimpsed earlier pucker her brow.

'And now?'

Glancing his way again, she shrugged.

'I think they should have a strip. The land's as flat as a table top so it wouldn't cost much to 'doze one, and although I wouldn't for the world wish accidents on any of the workers, they do happen and in cases like this we could airlift the injured men straight out rather than having to bring them into town and then airlift them. Every time they're moved, we put them more at risk of infection.'

'Well, now the company is bringing in more men to build their experimental power plant, maybe they will put in a strip.'

The lights were getting closer—and brighter—glowing in the blackness of the night.

'If it's not already planned, you could put it in your suggestions,' Neena told him, concentrating on how useful this stranger could be rather than the weird sensations he was causing in her intestines.

Or wondering whether the real reason he was here was to take her baby from her—to absorb her child—into the conglomerate that was 'the family'.

Theo's family.

'Suggestions?' he said, sounding so vague, anger surged inside her.

'*Isn't* that the job you were sent for?'

The words grated from her throat as she pulled up outside the camp office, noticing in her rear-vision mirror the flashing lights of the ambulance approaching in the distance. Slipping out of the vehicle, she grabbed her bag from the back seat and hurried into the well-lit but warm cabin.

'We covered them with clean sheets like you said, turned off the air-con and gave them a small dose of morphine,' an anxious-looking man told them as they walked in. He was hovering between two desks on which the injured men had been laid. 'We've a stretcher in the medical room but the light's better in here.'

Neena had set her bag down on the floor and opened it. Mak knelt beside her, silently congratulating her forethought. Burns victims lost heat rapidly, and with shock a likely side-effect of the trauma, they needed to be kept warm.

'One each?' he suggested as she handed him a suction device and an endotracheal tube.

'Suction, intubate then fluid.' She was muttering more to herself than to Mak.

'Large-bore catheters in both arms,' he said.

Although her confirming nod and quiet 'We need to allow good fluid access' told him she was thinking along the same lines as he was.

The ambulance attendants arrived as they worked, took in the situation at a glance and opened up the big bag they were carrying.

'We've a burns kit with treated gauze. Want us to cover the wounds?'

To cover or not to cover? It was a question that had tormented Neena in the burns cases she'd handled previously. She turned to Mak, knowing he'd have more experience.

'You're flying them out to a specialist unit,' he said, 'but you've two transfers before they leave here and another when they get to the city—opportunities each time for contamination. Let's cover.' He was competently siting a large-bore catheter in his patient's arm as he spoke. 'You've Ringer's in your bag?'

Neena nodded, concentrating on getting the catheter sited in her own patient's arm.

'That's the plane,' one of the ambos said, as a roaring overhead shook the shed that served as an office at the work site. 'They said they'd buzz us as they came in.'

'Okay, let's move them,' Neena suggested, as she attached tubing and a bag of fluid to the second catheter on her patient, adjusted the flow, then grabbed a transfer form to complete before the injured men left the site, noting down exactly what treatment they'd been given. 'You guys take them straight to the airfield. Dr Stavrou and I will see the other injured men.'

'Dr Stavrou?' one of the ambos queried, as the other helped Mak lift his patient onto a stretcher.

'Mak Stavrou, meet Pete and Paul, two of our crew of four local ambos,' Neena said, then she stood aside as Pete and Paul lifted her patient.

'He your replacement while you take maternity leave?' Paul asked, wheeling the patient towards the door.

Neena shook her head.

'I'll explain some other time, but for now, would you leave your burns kit here? I'll bring it back to town.'

Time enough for the townsfolk to learn why Mak Stavrou was here. And for him to learn the town's reaction! Not everyone was happy with the exploration crews, or the experimental power plant, but he'd find that out soon enough.

And *no one* in the town would be happy if they knew the suspicions she had about his visit! This was a town that protected its own, and Neena was definitely its own.

She hid a sigh bred from the frustration she often felt over this protective attitude, but they meant well, her town's people…

'Let's go see the others who were hurt,' she said to Mak, who was talking to the foreman.

'They're in the mess cabin, I'll take you over,' the foreman said, as Mak lifted the burns bag from her grasp, his fingers brushing hers in the exchange. 'They're not badly hurt,' the man continued, while Neena trailed behind the two men, telling herself she couldn't possibly have felt a reaction when the stranger's skin had brushed hers.

She was worried about the injured men, and uptight because she'd had this Mak Stavrou foisted on her. The twinge had been nothing more than tension.

'Some of the steam was still leaking from the pipes when they went over to drag their mates away but I'd say they're only superficial burns,' the foreman explained.

They *were* superficial burns, soon treated and dressed.

'Leave the dressings in place until Monday then come into town and we'll check the wounds and dress them again if necessary,' Mak told the three men.

They all agreed and thanked him, while Neena smiled to herself. In this case, Mak *was* the person with the most experience, but as far as these rough outback labourers were concerned, it was as natural to them as breathing to consider the male of the species as the main authority—the chief!

'Best if you're a boy,' she muttered, patting the bump as she made her way back to her vehicle. 'Life's a lot easier for men.'

CHAPTER TWO

BEST if you're a boy?

The phrase he'd heard Neena mutter hung in Mak's head as they drove away from the exploration site, but the weariness of the long drive out to Wymaralong was claiming him and he couldn't think clearly about the implication of the words.

'Do you not know the sex of your baby? I thought with regular scans most people found out quite early.'

Neena didn't take her eyes off the road, simply shaking her head by way of reply.

'I didn't want to know,' she said, and before she could explain the vehicle struck something and jolted to a stop, slewed across the road, airbags inflating so the world turned white.

'What the—!'

The muttered oath told him his companion was

conscious and as he fought his way out of the airbag he heard her door open.

'Are you all right?' she asked. 'Can you move your legs and arms? Coming on to dawn, I don't drive fast because I'm always wary of 'roos. I don't think we hit whatever it is hard enough for major injury but your side took the impact and the front wing is crumpled. Are your feet free?'

Mak wiggled his feet and moved his limbs. There was less foot room than there'd been earlier, but his feet weren't trapped.

'I'm conscious and feeling no pain so I assume I'm okay and, yes, my feet are free. What did we hit? I didn't see anything ahead of us and there certainly wasn't anything on the road as we came out.'

'It's a camel, I just looked. I'd heard there was a mob of them out here, but hadn't believed it. They're usually further west, around Alice and over in the Western Australia deserts. By the look of things it was already dead—maybe the ambulance hit it a glancing blow on its way back to town. The damage is on your side so I doubt your door will open. Here's a knife, can you cut your way free of the airbag? I'll phone a tow truck.'

He felt the knife press into his palm then heard

her move away, speaking quietly, no doubt
phoning for help, but when he made his way out
of the vehicle she wasn't on the phone. The headlights, still working on the driver's side, illuminated a macabre scene, the slight woman
kneeling by the big animal, talking not to it but
to a young calf that stood making bleating noises
at its mother, no doubt waiting for her to get up.

'She had this calf—the poor wee thing. See the
cord—it's not very old.'

The pain in the woman's voice pierced Mak's
heart and he heard his own voice saying, 'Don't
worry, we'll look after it.'

We?

He was here for a month and what did he know
about raising camels? Raising anything? Okay,
so he'd thought he'd be a father—once upon a
time—and he'd liked the idea, but his marital experience still rankled. It wasn't something he
was likely to repeat.

'I'd like to get a rope around his neck,' Neena
said.

Mak smiled to himself, feeling the words were
a great segue to his thoughts, then he realised she
was trying to hold the struggling baby camel.

Struggling baby camel? The animal was kicking its ridiculously long legs and the woman holding it was pregnant.

'Let go,' Mak ordered. Guessing she was about to argue, he added, 'If it kicks the baby, you'll be sorry.' He lifted it out of the way, standing up with it and wondering what to do next.

He supposed it was fate that the tow truck should arrive at that moment so he was illuminated by its headlights, standing in the middle of the road, a baby camel in his arms.

'You guys been having fun?' The tow-truck driver got out of his cab and surveyed the scene. 'Not your baby, is it, Neena?'

'It is now,' Neena told him, standing up and moving across to where the driver was examining the calf. 'We'd better put him in the back of my vehicle and get him out when we get to town. Can you drag the mother's body off the road a bit before you hitch up to my car, Nick? Oh, sorry, Nick, this is Mak—Mak, Nick.'

'New doctor in town, I heard,' Nick said as he offered his hand to Mak.

'Word gets around,' Mak said, shaking hands with the man, although it did puzzle him just how this had happened in the early hours of a Saturday morning, especially as the town had been deserted when he'd arrived.

He didn't puzzle over it long, putting the calf into the back of the vehicle then helping Nick wrap a chain around the dead camel and walking in front of the tow truck as it pulled the animal off the road and into bushes well off the track. Next, Neena's vehicle, with its badly damaged bull bar and left wheel arch, was attached for towing, and Neena, who had settled the calf in the back of her big four-wheel-drive, talking to it all the time, was persuaded to leave it for the drive back to town.

'Birds like ducks and geese attach themselves to humans if they don't have a mother—do you think camels might do the same?' she asked as she climbed into the tow vehicle, moving across the bench seat to make room for Mak in there as well.

'Patterning, don't they call it?' Nick said, and Mak's world became a dream again. Crammed into the cab of a tow truck as a brilliant dawn coloured the eastern sky, the smell of diesel fuel filling the air, and a slim, pregnant, beautiful woman squashed beside him, chatting on about the patterning habits of birds, stirring heat in his body again…

He'd put it down to tiredness and ignore it, that's what he'd do, but, exhausted as he was, the night was not over. As Nick pulled up outside the big old house and Mak wearily alighted, his hostess was already making plans.

'My office is the first room on the left, the computer's on the desk,' she said to Mak. 'Could you hop on the internet and see what you can find out about camel milk? The little one will need a drink. And Nick, if you wouldn't mind carrying it out to the stables. A rubber glove, that would do for a teat do you think, until I can get something sent out?'

'It's no use arguing,' Nick said to Mak, as Neena made her way to the back of her vehicle to release the calf. 'Once she's got a bee in her bonnet about something, there's no stopping her. I'd better catch up or she'll lift the damn thing out herself.'

Nick hurried after her while Mak wearily climbed the front steps. They felt as high as Everest, but as tiredness cramped his legs he had to wonder just how tired a pregnant woman must be feeling. Not that he intended using her office for the internet search on camel milk.

Was he really about to do that?

Yes, he was, but he'd use his laptop—that's if wireless worked out here. One day in four, she'd said—was that when it did work or it didn't?

He sighed, too tired and confused to think about such irrelevancies. Though wasn't the constitution of camel milk an irrelevance?

Not in Neena Singh's opinion!

He ate the sandwich as he searched the 'net, and even drank a cold cup of tea, making notes at the same time.

'Camel milk is lower in fat and lactose than cow's milk and higher in iron, potassium and Vitamin C,' he reported, after finding his way around the back of the house to what had obviously been stables at some time and entering the one that was brightly lit from within.

Neena, seated on the stable floor with the calf's head in her lap, looked up at him and smiled, although he was so far beyond smiles he wondered how she'd managed it.

'That's great. We can work out some kind of formula but to begin I've given him some newborn infant formula I had out here from when we were looking after an injured foal. There's no vet in town, you see, and the stables aren't used most of the time. Someone told me about rubber gloves and he seems to have taken to it because he drank quite a lot before he went to sleep.'

She held up a two-litre soft-drink bottle to which she'd attached a rubber glove, the fingers tied off so the thumb formed a soft teat.

Mak shook his head, although was feeding a camel calf through a rubber glove any more un-believable than the rest of the occurrences of the night?

'You should be in bed yourself,' he said, knowing if he didn't lie down soon he'd probably fall down but not wanting to portray such weakness in front of this apparently inexhaustible woman.

'I'll go soon. You go—have a shower and leave your clothes in a heap on the bathroom floor. Ned will take care of them for you. Grab some-thing to eat in the kitchen if you're hungry. You won't sleep otherwise.'

'And you're going to do what?' Mak demanded, sensing she had no intention of fol-lowing her own advice and going to bed.

'I'll doze here. From the moment I was pregnant I took up dozing. I can doze just about anywhere. And I don't want Albert waking up and finding himself alone.'

'Albert?'

She smiled at Mak and he felt a now familiar stirring deep inside him. Tiredness!

'He's got a noble look about him and I think Albert is a noble name, don't you? I did consider Clarence—Clarence the Camel, you know—but he might think that's a bit sissy when he grows up.'

'And Albert isn't?' Mak muttered, but not loudly enough for Neena to hear because right now he didn't want to get involved in an argument over the naming of a camel calf. Besides, she was talking again.

'When Ned gets up he'll rig up something for him, some way that Albert can feed on demand and some music or something to keep him company, but until then I'll stay here. There's straw and bags, I'll be perfectly comfortable.'

Mak knew he should argue, but with what— the on-demand feeding? What did he know? Her staying there? He doubted he'd budge her.

He walked away, but the image of her, sitting

on the floor, dirty and dishevelled, the camel's head on her lap, wouldn't go away.

Might never go away.

And *that* thought made him shiver…

Neena watched him go, her mind churning. A man who'd check out the constitution of camel milk in the early hours of the morning couldn't be all bad. But what if her suspicions were right—what if he'd come to take her baby from her, if not physically, then at least to persuade her to let the child be part of a family of which she had a very poor opinion?

She had to be wary of him—and not be taken in by little acts of kindness. Except that kindness, right now when she was feeling so terribly, terribly tired, seemed particularly important.

She studied the calf's funny face through teary eyes and told herself it was just pregnancy making her weepy, and thinking of the pregnancy—of *her* baby's welfare—she stretched out on the bag-covered straw and settled the calf so its legs were stretched away from her, then she patted Baby Singh, talked softly to him for a few minutes, telling him about the little camel he'd have for a playmate, wondering about family—

a concept not all that familiar to her, although deep down she knew that every child deserved to have a family.

But *that* family?

She wouldn't think about it now. Mak Stavrou was here for a month. She'd work it out before he left; right now she needed to sleep.

But every time she closed her eyes an image of her visitor was fixed to the inside of her eyelids and she was forced to study his face and try to work out just why it had so appealed to her.

It couldn't just be the strength of his facial bones, obvious because of the way his tanned skin stretched tautly over them, or the thick black eyebrows above dark hazel eyes, or the long nose kept from perfection by a thickening in the middle, or lips, pale but rimmed with a line of even paler skin so the sensuous fullness of them was emphasized.

'Oh, boy! Talk about trouble,' she told the sleeping Albert. 'Six months pregnant and I'm fantasising about a stranger. And not just any stranger—a Hellenic Enterprises stranger!'

As if one stranger from Hellenic Enterprises wasn't enough!

She patted the baby then curled her hands around the bump.

'It's okay,' she told him. 'We'll work it out. Together we can conquer the world.'

But the promise lacked conviction so she added, 'And if we can't there's always Ned and one thousand, four hundred and forty-two other Wymaralongites. Who needs family when we've got all of them?'

And on that note, she finally slept.

'How could you let her bring that animal home?' Ned demanded, when Mak, refreshed from four hours' solid sleep and now starving, made his way into the kitchen.

'You could have stopped her?' Mak enquired, and the old man shook his head.

'Nah! Never been any different, she hasn't,' Ned admitted, twiddling a knob on the coffee machine and pulling a mug out of a cupboard. 'Kittens, puppies, tortoises she picked up off the road, a duck one time, a galah with a broken wing—you name it, we've nursed it or reared it or sometimes had to bury it. But a camel—that's going too far. What's she going to do when it grows?'

'I imagine there are camel farms somewhere that will take it, or some tourist operator on the coast who uses them for beach rides. A sanctuary perhaps. I've never come across a baby camel before so am not sure about what one does with it when it grows.'

'Tourists riding on her camel? Yeah, I can see her letting that happen! People peering at it in a sanctuary? No, we're stuck with it.'

Ned handed Mak the mug of coffee, and waved his hand to milk and sugar on the table, somehow making the simple act a gesture of acceptance. Although Mak guessed Ned might be looking to him as an ally in some endeavour. Persuading Neena to part with her new pet?

Whatever it was, the man's suspicion of the previous night seemed to have vanished.

'Has she gone to bed?' Mak asked, and Ned nodded.

'Under protest, but I told her if she didn't sleep it would harm the baby—that usually works if ever you need to get her to rest.'

Definitely an ally, Mak realised.

'And the calf?'

'Happy as Larry,' Ned assured him. 'I've

rigged up a bag of old clothes and I've got formula in a plastic bottle inside it. The calf nudges and sucks and as long as the milk comes out he doesn't know he hasn't got a mother.'

Mak shook his head, aware this was becoming a habit, but it was obvious from Ned's conversation that he was just as dedicated to Neena's strays as she was. Or perhaps he was just used to being the one who had to work out how to feed them! A strange relationship, the wizened old man and the beautiful young woman—Mak would have liked to ask about it, but he didn't think the alliance between him and Ned was strong enough just yet.

Until Ned spoke again and he realised the alliance was less about the camel than about practical matters.

'Neena usually does a few hours on Saturday mornings at the surgery. Young Paula Gibbons is the nurse-receptionist on duty and I phoned her to say we're running late, but with Neena not long gone to bed I thought you might do it. Meet some people, talk to them about the town. You *are* a doctor?'

So Ned's suspicions were still alive and well,

Mak realised, and the old man had just been manoeuvring him towards this moment.

'I am and I'm happy to do it, but won't Neena—'

'Object? Sure she will. She'll mutter about people taking over her life but if we didn't do that occasionally she'd run herself ragged. Here, eat this before you go.'

Mak had been taking little notice of what Ned was doing as he talked, but now a beautiful omelette appeared in front of him, golden brown on the outside and within its fold melting cheese and fine slices of ham and tomato.

He ate, had a quick wash then followed Ned's instructions to the surgery, where Paula, a bright redhead, guided him through the patients for the morning, every one of whom asked him if he was Neena's locum for maternity leave and every one of whom had only good things to say about their local doctor.

Could someone so obviously not only respected but loved in this community be the devious woman he suspected she was?

Or was he only questioning his opinion of her because he was attracted to her?

Instantly attracted! This was something that had never happened to him in his entire life and therefore something of which he should be extremely wary—maybe even suspicious. Other experiences had taught him that attraction could make you forget common sense and for many years, as far as women were concerned, common sense had ruled his life.

And would continue to rule it. No matter how wonderful the townspeople thought this woman, he had to judge her for himself, and that would be impossible if he let the attraction get in the way.

He saw the last patient for the morning, had a chat to Paula—another Neena admirer—and headed back to the house. He wanted to go out to the geo-thermal site and speak to Bob Watson, head man out there, having ascertained the previous evening that Bob would be on duty today.

Neena woke to bright sunshine flooding through her window, and stared confusedly around her. She was on her bed, wrapped in her lightweight cotton robe, clean and naked, though she couldn't remember showering.

Or could she? Memories of Ned chasing her

out of the stables, threatening to turn the hose on her if she didn't go immediately. Somehow she'd made it to her room, stripped, showered—even washed her hair, from the feel of it, still slightly damp—then collapsed on the bed. But when? How long had she been asleep? And what was happening to her house guest? Ned might have turned him out by now.

Which, considering how she kept remembering the feel of his fingers touching hers as he'd taken the calf from her, was probably a good thing.

She'd think about the calf—about Albert!

She smiled and patted Baby Singh, picturing the camel calf's rubbery lips and curly eyelashes, his huge, soft, doe-like eyes.

'Such fun to have a pet again,' she told the baby, then she heaved herself off the bed and began to dress, anxious now to check that all was well in her small world. She hadn't phoned Brisbane to see how the burns victims were, or visited the hospital—though someone would have phoned if she'd been needed. And—

Her eyes fixed on the small digital clock beside her bed.

She'd missed morning surgery!

She shot out of her bedroom and blasted down the hall to the kitchen door.

'Ned, why didn't you wake me? It's lunchtime. My patients—'

'Have been seen. I brought back some notes in case you were concerned about any of them.'

Neena stared at the man who'd answered.

Her house guest, far from having been turfed out by Ned, had achieved the honour of being allowed access to the kitchen. In fact, he was sitting at the kitchen table—in *her* chair—eating lunch and chatting amiably to Ned.

'You saw my patients?' she demanded, anger and disbelief holding her motionless in the doorway.

'It's what I'm here for after all,' he said coolly. 'To gauge your workload, and even after less than twenty-four hours I can see you need another doctor.'

'So now you know that, maybe you can leave,' Neena snapped, then realised just how ungracious that sounded. But her kitchen, now she'd entered it, seemed to have shrunk, making the man seem closer than he was, the atmosphere thick and heavy.

'Not on the strength of one morning's surgery,' he said, so cool in the face of her rudeness she wanted to throw something at him. Something hard!

'Sit down and have your lunch.' This from Ned, and she knew his voice well enough to know he, too, was angry, but with her.

As well he should be!

'I'm sorry, that was terrible of me,' she muttered at Mak from the doorway. 'Yelling at you when I should be thanking you.'

He nodded a gracious acceptance of her apology, but she suspected he was laughing at her inside for his eyes were twinkling with delight, which made her mad again. But she *had* to enter the kitchen! For a start, she was starving. But her legs were heavy and stiff with dread because, for only the second time in her life, Neena was feeling physical responses to a man. Well, maybe not the second time—but only once before had they been as strong as this and that once had ended in heartache, pain and trouble.

'How's Albert?' she asked, directing the question at Ned, trying to ignore the other person in the room.

'Blooming,' the man she was trying to ignore replied. 'I've just been talking to him. He quite likes the Mozart but would prefer a little rock music from time to time.'

Neena frowned at the light-hearted comment. She didn't want to like this man—bad enough to be getting physical reactions from him, but liking him?

'Sit down and eat,' Ned told her, pulling a plate of cold meat and salad from the refrigerator and putting it down at the other end of the table from Mak, setting cutlery beside it and pouring her a glass of cold water.

So here she was, right opposite Mak Stavrou, where every time she looked up she'd see some bit of him, like how the dark hair on his arms curled around his watch. At least the table was long so she wouldn't be accidentally bumping his feet or have her knees knocking his...

Although not thinking about him was hard as once again came the memory of the previous night, of the touch of his hands on hers.

Ridiculous, fantasising about a stranger's touch!

'Lovely salad, Ned. Are these tomatoes from our garden?'

'You'll note she says "our",' Ned growled at Mak, 'though it's years since she dirtied her hands in the vegetable patch. Reckons looking after the roses is enough for her, not that roses take much looking after out here.'

'I noticed the rose gardens on my way to the stables,' Mak replied, smiling at Neena. 'My mother grows roses but I don't think I've ever seen such a wonderful display.'

'The dry climate means you don't get mildew or most of the bugs you get closer to the coast,' Neena replied, keeping the words crisp and impersonal, the mention of his mother reminding Neena of her doubts about why this man was really here.

Reminding her he could well be the enemy!

An enemy who had helped out this morning, she reminded herself. She asked him about the patients he had seen, and managed to eat most of her lunch while they discussed them.

'I'm going out to the drilling site this afternoon,' the man who was disrupting her life announced as he stood up from the table, rinsed his plate and put it in the dishwasher. 'I need to see some people and explain why I'm here. I want to talk to them about what they see as the impact on the township.'

'You might as well stay out there, then,' Neena told him. 'They're putting on a Christmas party for the town tonight. Every man and his dog will be there.'

Mak turned towards her and leaned against the kitchen bench.

'And every woman and her camel?'

Neena had to smile.

'Maybe not the camel, but as Ned is Father Christmas—yes, I know he's not a normal size Father Christmas but he does a great ho-ho-ho—we have to go.'

'Then I shall certainly stay for it,' Mak said with a smile that made moths flutter in her stomach and caused regret that she'd mentioned it.

He departed soon after and Neena went up to the hospital to check on patients there, then crossed to the retirement home to sit with her old friend Maisie for a while.

But Maisie's common sense, and their shared remembrances, failed to soothe the turbulence in Neena's chest. The arrival of the man from Hellenic Enterprises had thrown her into such a muddle she couldn't begin to think logically about him.

Or why he'd really come!

'Don't think too much,' Maisie said as Neena was leaving, and although Neena hadn't done more than mention Mak in passing, avoiding any discussion of him, she knew Maisie had picked up on her unhappy state of mind and had guessed he was the cause of it. 'Sometimes our instincts are our best guide.'

'Not mine!' Neena muttered, but only after she'd walked out of Maisie's room.

Back home she played with Albert for a while, walking him around the stall, talking to him, fondling his ears and scratching at his coat. But eventually she had to leave this safe retreat and get ready for the Christmas party.

Upstairs, she found a parcel on her bed and knew before she opened it what it would contain. Each year Ned made a trip to the two-dollar shop in Baranock and brought back Christmas shirts for the two of them, the surgery staff, the hospital staff and all the folk in the retirement home. This year his choice for her was a bright red singlet with a very tipsy reindeer on it, the deer's horns festooned with glittering streamers, its front feet holding a foaming mug of beer.

'Great! First time Mak Stavrou sees me dressed up and I'm wearing a tipsy reindeer!'

The words echoed around her bedroom, coming back to hit her with some force. Why on earth did it matter how she looked when Mak Stavrou saw her? her strong, grown-up and independent self demanded, but deep inside, another weak and feeble self knew that it did…

The site, usually three orderly rows of dongas, the demountable living huts now common in all mining areas of Australia, had been transformed. The dongas were strung with Christmas decorations, forming an aisle that led visitors down to a large marquee, brightly lit and covered in swathes of greenery the men had found somewhere in the bush. Christmas baubles and tiny fairy lights glittered in the leafy branches, making a magical grotto of a very ordinary large tent.

Was it fate that the first person Neena saw was Mak Stavrou or had she been looking for him? She hoped she hadn't been, but on the other hand she wasn't too keen to think it might be fate.

He was coming towards her with Bob Watson, the head of the geo-thermal exploratory crew.

'I'll go and get changed,' she heard Ned say behind her, and he promptly deserted her.

'Neena!' Bob greeted her, taking her hand and giving her a kiss on the cheek. 'Merry Christmas. You've already met Mak. Thanks on behalf of the company for taking him in. We could put him up out here but what's the point when he needs to see what you do in town and maybe take just a little work off your shoulders?'

Bob had barely said the words when he stepped away, holding up his hands in a mock surrender.

'No, don't rip up at me. I know you can handle *anything*.' He turned to Mak and added, 'And not only does she believe it, but she can! Wonderwoman, I call her.'

Neena knew she was probably as red as her singlet, and far from ripping up at Bob she was struck dumb, for Mak had pulled on a Santa hat and now that Neena looked around, she realised all the Hellenic work crew were wearing them. And whereas most people looked a trifle foolish in red pointy hats with white trim and a white bobble on the end, seeing Mak in his had suddenly evoked not memories of Christmases past but images of future Christmases, though why she should be seeing him beside a tree in her old house and, worse, seeing small children laughing up at him, she had no idea. In fact, the vision made her shiver, *and* miss whatever Bob was telling her.

'He suggested I take you through to the food tent,' Mak said, presumably picking up on her vacant state, but hopefully not on the cause of it.

Don't think too much, Maisie had told her, but when Mak put his hand on the small of her back to guide her through the throng, she ceased to think at all. *Couldn't* think! And didn't then throughout the evening, not when Mak piled ham and turkey on her plate, not when he led her to a blanket-covered bale of hay to sit and eat her dinner, not as she chatted about nothing very much and listened to him talk about cheap energy—about which he seemed particularly keen—and especially not when he led her out of the marquee to where a dance floor had been laid on the desert sands, and suggested she might dance with him.

'Because you're really the only woman I know

in town,' Mak told her. 'Apart from Paula, whom I met this morning but who seems to be attached to a very large farmer.'

So she danced with Mak beneath the stars—with a stranger to whom she was attracted—a stranger that the few brain cells still operating in her head warned her to avoid.

At all costs!

Don't think too much, she reminded them, hoping they'd calm down, because dancing with Mak was like dancing on a cloud, high above the real world, the bright light of the stars scattering magic all around them.

Of course it had to end. Sirens approaching from the distance told them not that a disaster was at hand but that Santa had arrived, not in a sled drawn by reindeers, or even leaping kangaroos, but in the local fire engine.

'At least it's red,' Mak remarked as Neena eased out of his arms and turned to watch the arrival.

He didn't sound any happier than she felt, but maybe she was imagining that. Or maybe he just liked dancing and he didn't know anyone else…

He still had one arm around her shoulder, but as excited children surged forward to grab the sweets Santa was throwing from his perch atop the fire engine, Mak touched the bump—very gently at first then settling his hand on it.

And as they'd been dancing with it pressed against him Neena could hardly object, although when he murmured, 'Next year you'll have someone special with whom to share your Christmas,' she felt a wave of sadness sweep over her. Yes, it would be good to have a baby in the house for Christmas, but right now the two of them as a family, even with Ned and Maisie added, seemed a little meagre.

Neena and Mak were separated by the crush of people moving to see Santa and though she talked and laughed with all those present, the magic had gone out of the evening. Until later when she and Ned—now Ned again—were about to leave and Mak caught up with her, guiding her into a shadowy spot outside the marquee.

His touch had started tremors in her limbs and shivers up her spine—ridiculous, she knew, but how to stop them?

'Bob's offered me a bed in his donga,' Mak began. So that was how to stop tremors and shivers—they disappeared immediately! 'Just for tonight so I can go out with him in the morning to see another site where they are drilling.'

Neena could only stare at him—her brain once again gone AWOL. *Surely* she couldn't have been thinking he'd been going to kiss her!

Shivers, tremors—of course she had been. Or if not thinking it, then hoping…

'That's okay,' she managed, her words cutting across his explanation that he hoped to be back in town by lunchtime. 'The house is never locked so we'll see you when we see you.'

She walked away, her legs feeling ridiculously weak and trembly. Must be all the dancing…

Mak watched her join up with Ned in a group of people, then after kisses and hugs and various other forms of farewell, the pair of them walked into the darkness. Was it because they'd danced that the last thing he'd wanted to do in that shadowy corner was tell her his plans for the following day? What he'd *wanted* to do—so badly he'd barely restrained himself—had been to kiss her. Hold her in his arms and kiss the breath right out of her.

He lifted his arms and raked his hands through his hair, cursing silently in Greek as he tried to make sense of a situation that was fast spiralling out of control. He'd been here less than twenty-four hours and the woman he was supposed to be checking out—a woman of whom he was still suspicious—had woven a spell around him.

Had he forgotten how perfidious women could be? Forgotten his vow never to become involved—emotionally involved—with one of them again? Where was his head, where were his brains?

He strode out into the darkness, thinking a brisk walk might sort things out, knowing the lights were bright enough to guide him back to the camp. But with every stride some memory of Neena intervened. Bob telling him what a great doctor she was, and how she attacked any problem with grit and determination, sorting out not only the townspeople's illnesses but the tangles some of them made of their lives.

Now an image of Neena with Albert's head on her knee popped into Mak's head, and he heard her quiet voice soothing the little orphaned animal to sleep. Would a woman who took in stray animals deliberately get pregnant?

He shook his head and picked up his pace, wondering what on earth he was doing out here in this godforsaken desert land. Then he heard the sound of carols drift through the hot night air and knew.

It was about Christmas, and Christmas was about family.

CHAPTER THREE

MAK returned as Neena was eating her lunch. She'd had a good sleep-in, for once undisturbed by any emergency, but Sunday had brought no relief from the problem that was Mak. He'd visited her dreams, a tall, dark-haired man in a Santa cap, teasing her so her body had heated in her sleep and she'd tossed and turned.

Now he was here in person, chatting on to Ned about the drilling site and geo-thermal plant and totally oblivious of the ructions he'd caused in the night—ructions he was still causing…

She had to escape him!

'I'm off to the hospital,' she told him. 'Nick dropped off a loaner car for me yesterday after-noon. I know you worked yesterday morning, but there's no need for you to hang around with me today. Ned can show you around the town, not that there's much to see, though most tourists are interested in the bore head. Our artesian bore was one of the first sunk in Western Queensland.'

He'd lost her! The seeds of the tentative, if not friendship then working relationship Mak thought they'd achieved, not to mention the rapport he'd sensed as they'd danced last night, had been washed away in the bright light of day.

'I'll come to the hospital with you. If your week doesn't acknowledge Sundays, why should mine?'

Dark eyes studied him—wary? Suspicious? Then she shrugged her shoulders as if he was of no importance whatsoever.

Which in her mind was probably true, so why should it bother *him*? Because they'd danced beneath the stars? Was she regretting that as much as he was? From his side it was because it had thrown him off track—made him forget just why he was here, which was to persuade this woman to let her child be part of his family, and hope that the child could help to reunite and rebuild his family.

'If you like,' she said, pushing aside her half-eaten meal and standing up. 'I'll pop down and visit Albert and meet you at the car in ten minutes. That suit you?'

She wasn't really asking, so he didn't reply, puzzling instead over the change in her manner.

Did it matter?

Not really as far as his official job was concerned, but if he was to persuade her to let Helen and his mother be part of the baby's life, then he had to win her trust.

How he was supposed to persuade her to vote the baby's shares with Helen was a whole different ball game, but he was sure trust had to come into it!

But how did he go about winning trust? He was a doctor, for heaven's sake, people usually trusted him automatically—he didn't have to go out of his way to prove himself.

He carried his plate over to the counter by the sink, where Ned was leaning, a broad smile on his grizzled face.

'Prickly little thing, ain't she?'

Mak glared at him, not needing the snide observation to bring home the fact that Neena Singh had definitely gone off him!

'The hospital has twenty beds, but they're rarely full.'

Neena passed on this riveting fact as the man

settled into the beaten-up loaner four-wheel-drive and did up his seat belt. Determined to keep things on a purely professional basis and to forget—for the moment—why he was here and, more difficult, the way he was affecting her, she continued in the same vein.

'The flying surgeon used to operate here but with the town's decline in population—before the exploratory teams turned up—and the widening of the road between here and Baranock, he now operates there once a month, so any surgical patients from Wymaralong will spend their first twenty-four hours post-op in Baranock then come back to us.'

'And are people obliging enough to save their acute appendicitis until the surgeon's due to visit?'

Neena swung to face him, frowning at the slight smile—smug, surely—on his face. The smile focussed attention on his lips—lips that had already featured in her dreams, lips she'd thought for one fleeting moment last night might actually kiss her!

Professional, she reminded herself, turning into the tree-lined drive that led up to the low-set hospital.

'The flying doctors take the acute appendicitis cases straight to a bigger hospital. The flying surgeon does elective stuff, carpal tunnel, hip replacements, hernias—even in the city I imagine patients have to wait for surgery.'

'Too long,' Mak agreed, so honestly that Neena found herself liking him again.

Well, liking a colleague was okay, wasn't it?

'At St Kit's we try to keep the waiting lists as short as possible, but I doubt we'll ever have the facilities or the staff in any city hospital to reduce them to zero.'

'I've read about the problems,' she said, pulling up in the shade of one of the spreading pepper trees. 'In fact, the more I read the more I think our services are better in the country—for some things. Having to send people away for operations—and for childbirth—is disappointing, but it's unavoidable these days.'

He was coming around the car towards her, a tall man in lightweight cotton trousers and a dark green polo shirt. Did he wear green to make his eyes seem greener?

Or would a man like him not realise that?

She didn't have a clue what kind of man he

was, and probably would never know him well enough to guess, and *that* thought, as he fell in beside her to walk into the hospital, sent a twinge of sadness through her heart.

Stupid heart! This was a man who'd come into her life less than forty-eight hours ago—what could she be thinking?

'We've a terrific bunch of nurses at the moment—in fact, they've always been top class. For a long time, before I came back here, they put up with locums coming and going, and virtually ran the hospital and catered for the townspeople's medical needs themselves.'

She took the two steps in a stride and stopped at the top as a middle-aged woman in dark blue long shorts and a paler blue shirt came out of the front door, a door already festooned with Christmas decorations.

'I know you were out dancing last night so I phoned Ned and told him to tell you we didn't need you,' she scolded, and Neena, feeling about six years old in the face of Lauren's disapproval, hurriedly introduced Mak.

'We do need another doctor—even without the power plant going ahead, the town's population could carry two GPs,' Lauren said, shaking Mak's hand and sizing him up at the same time. 'Come on in, I'll give you the tour. You.'

She turned to Neena.

'You can make the tea. I bought some more of those lemon-flavoured decaffeinated teabags for you so don't think you can sneak a real one because I'll smell it.'

Neena scowled at her. 'Never fall pregnant in a country town where every citizen feels impelled to count your caffeine intake every day,' she grumbled at Mak.

'I'll try not to,' he said, a teasing smile twisting those mesmeric lips. 'Caffeine addict, were you?'

'Was she ever.' Lauren answered for her. 'The worst! Coffee morning noon and night, then she gets pregnant and tries to convince us all that tea has no caffeine in it—as if we'd fall for that!'

Mak was once again struck by the protective attitude towards Neena—a loving protection that he assumed she must have earned. He remembered the conversation as they'd driven up to the hospital—remembered her saying she'd come *back* to town.

'Did she grow up here that you're all so

watchful of her?' he asked Lauren as the straight back with the long black plait dangling down it disappeared through a side door.

'She did. Her father came out here from India at a time when it was nearly impossible to get doctors in the country. He was newly married and wanted to build a better life for his family, but sadly his wife died in a car accident when Neena was four, and she was the only family he had.'

'She and the townsfolk,' Mak suggested, and Lauren smiled.

'It took a while. We're not a trusting lot, out here in the bush, but he was so good to everyone, and then his wife dying so, yes, the town took him to their hearts. Then— But you're here to see the hospital, not hear the history of the town. As you can see, we've four four-bed wards straight off the central corridor and one more right at the back, but the back three are permanently closed. Mr Temple here—' she led him into the ward on the right '—is in while Neena gets his medication sorted. He goes back home—he lives out of town—and forgets to take his tablets, then takes too many—'

She broke off as she reached the bed of the ward's only occupant.

'Mr Temple, this is Dr Stavrou. He's here to help out for a while.'

'While Neena has her baby?' the old man asked. 'You know if it's a boy she's going to call it after me?'

'Call it Mr Temple?' Lauren teased, and the patient glared at her.

'You know I've got a name, it's on me chart, I just don't hold with this modern habit of everyone calling everyone by their first names as if they're all best mates.'

'I quite agree,' Mak told him, surreptitiously checking the chart to see what the man's name was, but the scrawl was indecipherable. Surely not Clarence. If Neena wouldn't call a camel Clarence she wouldn't—

'It's Charles, if you're trying to read it upside down,' Mr Temple said. 'That's a perfectly proper name for a baby. It's a real name, not a made-up one like Autumn.'

'Mr Temple's great-granddaughter is called Summer,' Lauren explained. 'And his granddaughter is expecting her second one, but she's only teasing you, Mr Temple, about calling it Autumn. Maybe if she has a boy she'll call him Charles.'

'Can't have a whole class of Charleses in the same class at the school in five years' time!' the patient grumbled.

Mak listened to the conversation while a strange feeling of contentment swept through him. Wasn't this what he'd envisaged when he'd begun to study medicine—spending time with patients, quality time, not the rushed politeness of the ER? Of course, it was impossible to think that this situation could be re-created in a city practice or city hospital.

Or could it?

Lauren was leading him out of the ward and into the one across the passage where two middle-aged women were sitting up in bed knitting, metal walking frames by their beds suggesting they might be post-op hip replacements.

'The terrible twosome,' Lauren introduced them. 'Marnie and Phyllis. Twins, though you wouldn't know it to look at them, and determined that if one experiences something the other must as well. Marnie fell at the clothesline and broke her ankle, had to be airlifted out so it could be pinned and plated and she's back here until we get her weight-bearing on it, and Phyllis, not to be outdone, broke her leg last week. Simple fracture of the tib and fib, Neena set it here. We've only kept Phyllis over the weekend because she's having trouble with crutches and the walking frame will be hard for her to manage at home.'

'And because I'm company for Marnie and with shearing next week I won't get the layette finished for Neena's baby if I have to go home,' Phyllis told him, holding up the tiny garment— in bright purple wool—that she was knitting.

Marnie's wool was green and Mak wondered if politeness would decree Neena's baby had to wear the garments being knitted out of kindness and no doubt love.

'Green and purple?' he said to Lauren as she led him into the big kitchen at the back of the building.

'They're not still knitting, are they?' Neena demanded, picking up on the conversation immediately. 'Honestly, Lauren, can't you tangle the wool in the walking frames?'

'My baby had to wear a bright orange jumpsuit knitted by the twins, and it was midsummer at the time, so live with it. Put the things on when you know the twins'll be in town on mail days, and the rest of the time dress him however you want.'

She waved the teapot at Mak and at his nod poured a mug of tea, pushing a plate of biscuits towards him.

'Does everyone in this town consider you're having a boy?' Mak asked Neena, who was sipping distastefully at her aromatic drink.

'We're kind of assuming it because of the general nuisance value,' Lauren said.

'Boys being more annoying than girls?' Mak guessed, deciding a second biscuit, each bite rich with chocolate pieces, wouldn't go astray.

'When they're younger, definitely,' Lauren said. 'Girls rarely think of taping kites to their backs and jumping off the garage roof to see if they can fly.'

'He only broke one leg,' Neena put in. 'And you have to admit, you worry a lot more about your girls now they're older.'

'All teenagers are a worry,' Lauren decreed. 'You got kids?'

This last was directed at Mak and he knew enough about hospital gossip to realise this was also an 'are you married' question.

'No kids,' he said, deliberately not taking the bait, though again feeling a faint twinge of what couldn't possibly be regret. After Rosalie, his distaste for the marriage experience had been so strong he'd decided it was something he would never repeat. But kids? Back then, he'd been excited about the prospect of a baby, about being a father…

'Lucky you,' Lauren said, and he could feel the next question hovering on her lips, but at that moment there was a loud crash and Neena and Lauren rushed from the room.

'Phyllis, didn't I tell you to buzz me before you tried to use the crutches?' Lauren was saying when Mak arrived at the scene of the accident— a fall on the veranda outside the kitchen.

'Yes, well, Marnie reckoned he looked a bit like The Rat and I had to check.'

Neena and Lauren had her back on her feet and were settling the crutches under her armpits, both of them looking slightly flustered. But Phyllis had no intention of moving, not until she'd studied Mak's face intently enough to make a judgement, finally shaking her head.

'Nah, she's wrong. The Rat had the charm thing going—sparkly eyes whenever he looked at any woman. Smile about to pop out, always there ready on his lips. This bloke looks okay. Solid!'

She nodded at Neena as if her judgement was approving something, though what Mak didn't like to think, then, with Lauren by her side, she started back to bed.

'Pity she didn't break her wrist when she fell,' Neena muttered as he followed her back into the kitchen.

'Nice attitude for a doctor,' he told her, and she turned to frown at him, studying him.

'She couldn't knit with a broken wrist,' she said, but Mak had the strangest sensation that knitting was the last thing on her mind. He'd figured out 'The Rat' was none other than his dead nephew, but from the look of disappointment on Neena's face, she, too, had found no resemblance.

Shouldn't that be good?

'Phyllis thought I looked okay,' he told her, and won a half-smile.

'Phyllis thinks all men look okay—she's a fifty-seven-year-old spinster—she and Marnie run the family property. Marnie was married at one time, but to another Rat, but that doesn't mean they judge all men by his behaviour. In fact, at one time, Phyllis rather hoped she might become my stepmother, but my dad was hung up on my mother even after she died and that was never going to happen.'

Mak shook his head—it was definitely becoming a habit. 'Are all country towns this—with everyone seeming to know everyone else's business? Do you ever get any privacy?'

Neena smiled at him and patted the small neat baby bump protruding under her T-shirt.

'I must have at least once, mustn't I?' she said, and although she spoke lightly, the smile had slid off her face and the sadness in her eyes made him want to hug her.

Hug her? A woman pregnant by his nephew—the nephew commonly known in town as The Rat? A woman who might have deliberately become pregnant? More to the point, a woman who carried a rifle in her car? He'd seen it there when he'd put Albert inside in the early hours of Saturday morning.

Hugging just wasn't on the agenda.

Not now, and not ever.

Though hadn't he held her in his arms when they'd been dancing? Even touched her bump? And she hadn't objected to that!

'Where next?' he asked, taking another biscuit

because chocolate was good energy food, and they were the best biscuits he'd ever tasted.

'Retirement units next door—it's not quite a nursing home, but some of the people living there are getting on a bit and Maisie, one of the oldest, has been having breathing problems. It's congestive heart failure but…'

'But?' Mak echoed, when it became clear Neena wasn't going to expand on the subject.

'Come and meet her, but be warned, she's another lifelong spinster with an eye for single men, and although you ducked that question from Lauren earlier, can I assume you *are* single?'

'I am,' Mak replied, and found himself wishing she was asking for personal reasons, although he knew full well that wasn't the case. He was going to be working with her—it was natural she'd want to know something of his background, and marital status was part of that background.

'Maisie will be delighted,' Neena told him, her smile back again—a more healthy smile this time.

She stood up and led him off the back veranda of the hospital and across a gravelly strip of land where nothing grew towards a newish building, brick with a green tiled roof.

'The local service clubs got together to build it, and having it close to the hospital means we can share the staff. All meals are supplied, although some of the units have small kitchens so the residents can be self-sufficient if they like. Being Sunday, there'll be a barbeque late this afternoon if you want to stay for it.'

She led the way into the cool building, and along a wide corridor towards a big open room. Four women and two men were sitting in there, watching television or reading. Neena spoke to a young man in dark blue shorts and a paler blue shirt, the male version of the uniform Lauren had been wearing.

'Maisie?'

'In the greenhouse,' he said, and though he looked enquiringly at Mak, Neena didn't introduce him, leading him out of the room and further down the hall.

'The building was designed to be eco-efficient. Like most western buildings, it has an evaporative air-cooling unit on the roof, and the greenhouse provides shade from the western sun. It also gives the residents who are interested something to do, looking after the plants.'

She opened a door that led directly into the shade-cloth covered room—no, it was larger than a room, more the size of a village hall. And everywhere were orchids in full bloom, long stems of them bending across the narrow passage between the shelves of plants.

'But they're beautiful,' Mak said, noticing for the first time a woman in a wheelchair down the end of the greenhouse.

'They are, and a lot of them have been propagated from plants Maisie brought from her home when she shifted in, and she's the one who's taught the others how to care for them. Right now I'd guess she's tagging the flowering plants she wants to go on display in the hospital and in the common room here. Hi, Maisie, I've brought you a visitor.'

'Nice-looking man, from what I hear,' the old voice croaked. 'Come closer so I can take a look at you.'

Mak walked obediently closer, hoping shock wasn't registering on his face as he saw how old the orchid cultivator was. Rheumy brown eyes were almost lost in a maze of wrinkles, while toothless gums shone in her wide smile.

'I'm Mak Stavrou,' he said, bending over to take her hand, and without thinking, to lift it to his lips for a gentle kiss.

'Mac like in MacKenzie?' she asked, letting her hand linger in his.

'No, spelled with a K and short for Makarios, a Greek name meaning blessed. My parents had a daughter first and, being traditional Greeks, thought the family needed a boy. It took a while, hence the name, although my sister turned out to be the one who followed in my father's footsteps.'

'I hope you are blessed,' Maisie said, and Mak heard the wheeze in her voice and realised that even this short conversation had tired her.

'Is there anything you need?' Neena asked, and when Maisie shook her head, they stayed a little longer, Neena telling him the names of the various orchids, pointing out which ones were native to Australia, showing off Maisie's work in a way that was obviously pleasing to her but not exhausting her.

'Is she on diuretics? Heart medication?' Mak asked when they'd said their goodbyes and left the greenhouse, taking an outside door and heading across the car park towards the car.

'Not any more,' Neena said, the sadness so evident in her voice Mak had the urge to hug her again.

'Why not?'

He had to ask.

'She doesn't want it. She says it's time to go and she doesn't want her body rattling with pills and potions when she turns up at the Pearly Gates. That's a direct quote, I might add. She's a great believer in the Pearly Gates. She's also quite sound in her mind, so I have to respect her wishes.'

'But she seems to have a lot of life in her yet and she loves the orchids—wouldn't she want to see them flower again?'

Neena turned towards this man who had come so suddenly into her life and was now disrupting it quite enough without arguing over Maisie's medication—a subject that already tormented her.

'She's one hundred and five, Mak,' she said. 'She's seen the orchids bloom enough. And don't think I haven't been trying to persuade her otherwise. She's been part of my life for ever. She's Ned's mother, and she was our housekeeper when my mother died, passing the job on to Ned when she retired.'

'She brought you up?' Mak said softly, and Neena nodded, the sadness she felt almost overwhelming her.

'And right at the end I disappointed her—great, isn't it?' she said bitterly, then she strode away.

Perhaps her pregnancy hadn't been deliberate. The thought struck Mak as he followed her back to the car, his steps slowing as hers speeded up.

But she was a doctor—she'd have a supply of morning-after pills in her surgery, every GP would have them these days. So even if becoming pregnant *had* been accidental, continuing with the pregnancy had been deliberate.

And persuading Theo to include the unborn baby in his will? Had he *not* been careful? Had she worked on that?

Just because everyone in town thought she was the bee's knees, it didn't mean she wasn't as devious as most women. Look at Helen, at his mother, at his ex-wife—all past masters in the art of getting their own way.

'You not ready to move on?' Neena called, and he realised his forward progress had stopped altogether, his mind lost in the past. No, he wasn't married, as he had told Lauren earlier, but he had been once, persuaded into marriage by a woman whom he'd believed was carrying his child.

When the pregnancy hadn't progressed—an apparent miscarriage—they'd struggled on for a while, Mak believing marriage was for keeps, but six months later his wife had announced she was in love with his best man and wanted a divorce.

The fact that his best man had been a corporate raider who had earned more in a month than Mak had earned in a year probably had nothing to do with it, but he'd wished he'd brought the two of them together earlier. It would have saved a lot of emotional torment of the 'where did he go wrong' type, not to mention a lot of fuss and embarrassment.

'Have you ever been married?'

The question from the woman leaning negligently against the car fitted so well into his thoughts he wondered about ESP, then hoped she didn't really have it as he'd been having some unlikely thoughts about her.

'Phyllis not into divorced men?' he asked, and she smiled at him.

'I don't think it's an issue for her. In fact, I don't know why I asked. I suppose because you're older than the young unmarried male schoolteachers and nurses we get out here. Except for them, we don't get a lot of single men coming to town, so it isn't only Phyllis you'll have to watch out for.'

'Surely having the work crews here helped redress the imbalance,' Mak said, then realised he'd probably hurt her as a fiery blush swept into her cheeks and she climbed hurriedly into the car.

CHAPTER FOUR

MAK joined her, glancing sideways, wanting to judge her mood—wanting to apologise, but how?

Her profile could have been carved from stone, so little did it reveal, but as they left the hospital grounds she turned left, off the road they'd driven in on, taking him in a direction he didn't recognise. To his surprise there was a hill in what he'd thought a dead flat landscape—a rough and rocky hill, the road winding up it to a lookout at the top.

Neena parked the car and got out, determined to get things settled with this man. For the good of the town she had to work with him, so best things got sorted out right now.

'This is our local lookout—that's a lake fed by the bore below us, and up here, a few years back, the local council received some arts funding and had a camp of sculptors visit the town, producing the artworks you see along this walk.'

Her house guest looked bemused but she didn't care. This was a favourite place of hers, a place her father had always brought her when she'd been cross or out of sorts, frustrated by the way her world was working. Up here, with the wide red desert sands stretching to the horizon in all directions, she would find peace steal into her soul and her world would return to rights.

She doubted that would happen this afternoon, but at least she felt the presence of her father here—some family support!

She led Mak past the big sculptures, The Working Man, The Rainbow Serpent, The Shearer and The Drover, to the small statue at the end, a very freeform figure of a mother and a child, carved from the red sandstone of the hill and called simply Serenity. Not that she'd tell Mak that!

She waved him down onto the seat beside the statue.

'I was wondering,' she began, her heart hammering against her ribs at the temerity of what she was about to ask. 'Mak Stavrou, Greek name, Hellenic Enterprises, Greek business—is there a connection?'

She watched him as she spoke, and saw the frown that puckered his forehead. Would he lie?

And would she know if he did?

Probably not, but she knew she couldn't go on pretending that she believed his story when she had so many doubts. Doubts she wanted to dispel—just as she wanted him to assure her she was wrong…

Mak considered what to say, sorry he hadn't talked about this earlier—yet what time had there been? As they'd treated burns victims together? As they'd danced beneath the stars?

He remembered that brief interlude with a pang, while he considered how to answer. No way could he lie. Even if she asked him to leave town forthwith, he had to tell the truth. It was better that way—no more deceit, no more discomfort about not being fully honest with her.

'I was Theo's uncle.'

'And his mother sent you?'

'No way! Well, the job came through her and it's a genuine job—the company wants to help the town, and I have the qualifications to look at the medical services. As to the rest, well, the baby will be family, he will be my sister's grandchild, my mother's great-grandchild.'

She turned towards him, but it was only a glance—a frowning glance.

'Is it the family tie or the fact that Theo, for whatever reason, willed the baby shares in the company? Which brings you here?'

Mak hesitated, wondering how to answer, again feeling that it was essential there was honesty between them.

'We're Greek, so family ties are very important, and to be perfectly honest with you, Neena, the family part of it was what prompted me to come. I'd like to think the baby knows his family—that he knows we'll always be there for him—and for you, of course. Personally, I'd like to help you plan for his future—that's probably something to do with the fact that I'm now the senior male in the family. As you might have gathered, family is something I feel strongly about.'

'Is there a but following that very touching admission?' she asked and he glimpsed the steel in this woman who carried such a load of responsibility on her own—steel she must need from time to time.

Truth! he reminded himself, making a helpless gesture with his hands before answering.

'There is now,' he admitted. 'The share situation has become complicated. How much do you know about the shares?'

He saw her frown deepen, then she shrugged.

'I had a letter from a solicitor saying Theo had been killed in an accident and had left his shares in the company to the baby. I was shocked to hear about his death—he was too young to die so senselessly. I filed the letter away somewhere and thought no more about the share thing.'

He was too young to die so senselessly? Not 'I was devastated,' which was surely what she'd have said if she'd loved him? Was his suspicion that the pregnancy might have been her idea correct? Why did it keep recurring?

Dragging his mind off that tangent—it was something he could think about later—he asked, 'You've only received one letter?'

She looked at him, still frowning, definitely perturbed.

'No, there might have been more, but I've been busy so I just put them all into a folder to look at some other time—after all, the baby isn't here yet, so the shares can't be of any importance to him.'

How to explain? Mak took a deep breath.

'Not to him, but they are important within the context of the company,' he began, although he doubted she would care about a company of which she knew so little. 'The share situation became complicated when my father died before Theo. Although my father's sisters' sons have always been part of the company, Theo was the designated heir.'

Mak hesitated, wondering how she would take the revelation he was about to impart. If monetary gain had been her aim all along, she would surely be delighted, although probably too smart to show it.

He took a deep breath and told her.

'Your unborn baby is now the majority shareholder of Hellenic Enterprises.'

She stared at him, then shook her head and stood up, her body stiff with tension as she paced around the stone statue nearest to them. 'I can't even begin to consider the implications of that, although now all the strange offers I got from Theo's mother make more sense.'

Neena folded her arms across her chest and glared down at Mak.

'She was trying to buy me—trying to buy my

votes—and I thought it was just the baby she wanted!'

He wanted to protest, to tell her Helen wanted the child to be family just as he did, but how could he when the complication of the shares—and Helen's fears they'd lose control of the company—made the situation look so bad?

'The baby *will* be her grandchild,' he reminded Neena. 'He or she will be all she has left of her son. He will be family.'

'He will not necessarily be part of *that* family!' Neena spat the words at him then took another turn around the statue.

'It's no good,' she finally announced. 'I just can't get my head around it at the moment. I'll think about it all some other time.'

She stared out over the lake. The revelation about the number of shares—could the bump beneath her rib cage really be the majority shareholder of the company?—was too startling to take in right now, although she was more suspicious than ever of the man who had come into her life.

The same man she'd thought might kiss her.

She felt the presence of the stone woman and child close beside her, but today the serenity she usually found in this place was missing, not only because of the conversation but because her awareness of Mak's body claimed all her senses, tingling in her skin, prickling at the short hairs on the back of her neck, heating her body, although the sun was sinking towards the horizon and a cooling breeze was whispering across the lake.

Was she mad?

How could she possibly be attracted to this man?

And if it *was* attraction, then surely common sense dictated she send him away—far, far away?

Now she knew who he was and why he was really here, she'd be justified in asking him to leave.

But how could she send him away if the town could gain from his visit—and the town *would* gain if he was genuine in his desire to assess the needs.

If…

'That family'. She spoke of his family in the same way Helen had spoken of her—'that woman'. The conversation, in spite of the fact that there was now no deceit between them, had made Mak feel distinctly uneasy. If he had a scrap of common sense he'd leave town right now, riding off into the sunset—or maybe it was the sunrise from here—like a defeated cowboy in the old movies. But the thought of leaving town held no appeal whatsoever.

And if he was perfectly honest with himself, his reluctance had less to do with the shares, or Helen and her grandchild—even his mother's grief—and more to do with a growing fascination with the woman by his side, a woman to whom he felt an undoubted attraction, but, worse than that, in whom he felt a deepening interest. She was beautiful, yes, and that accounted for the attraction, but beyond the beauty he sensed a strength and determination and commitment that made her something special.

But hadn't he thought Rosalie special at one time?

If he thought about it deeply enough, he knew he'd probably have to answer no. She had been beautiful and intelligent and fun to be with, certainly physically attractive to him, but special?

He let out a long sigh. As if this particular woman, special or not, would want anything to do with *him* of all people!

'The sun's setting, we have to shift to the other side of the statues,' the special woman said, standing up and walking away from him.

He followed, but didn't walk far, for as he passed the strange carved shape labelled Serenity, he saw the colours of the sunset, brilliant, vivid stripes of purple and vermillion, of hot orange and a lurid pink, all somehow working together to paint a vision the likes of which he'd never seen.

'That's unbelievable,' he managed to murmur as the colours faded to mauves and dusky rose.

'We do good sunsets,' his companion said, still watching the colours change, her back straight, her body still, as if movement might spoil the magic of the moment.

The following day began predictably enough. After breakfast, bacon, eggs and sausages served by Ned, who had obviously never heard of cholesterol, and a visit to Albert, who had to be the funniest-looking small animal Mak had ever seen—all legs and lips—Neena took him to the surgery.

'As you no doubt discovered on Saturday, we've two consulting rooms,' she'd said, as she introduced him to 'the girls' who ran the practice on weekday mornings, 'so what if you take all the male patients? A number of them will be thrilled to have a male doctor to talk to.'

Mak nodded, still trying to get his head around a medical receptionist who looked at least eighty and a practice nurse who wasn't much younger.

And so they worked through the morning; the three men from the power plant were the first patients he saw, their wounds healing well. After examination, he had them re-dressed by the septuagenarian nurse.

They broke for lunch, freshly cut sandwiches, platters of fruit, tubs of yoghurt, provided by a cheerful, fresh-faced young woman from the local café.

'If you want something hot, you only have to tell me,' she said to Mak. 'Dr Singh, not Neena but her dad, liked a hot lunch.'

As Mak had by now worked out that the previous Dr Singh had been dead for at least eighteen years and this young woman looked about that age, he did wonder about this information.

Wondered aloud!

'We've always got our lunch from the café,' Mildred, the receptionist, told him. 'And the same family still run it. Young Keira will take it over from her parents one day. Her brothers aren't interested. They're on the rodeo circuit.'

Mak had to smile.

'Imagine growing up where going on the rodeo circuit was a job opportunity!' he said, as Neena came to join them in the lunchroom.

'Or helicopter mustering,' she said. 'Have you had your lunch?'

She was wrapping a couple of sandwiches in a paper napkin as she asked the question, then she found a cool-bag and popped them in, added a tub of yoghurt and a bottle of water and headed back out the door.

'Come on,' she said from the doorway. 'You can drive while I eat.'

'But the afternoon patients?' Mak queried.

'They'll wait. They know I only go out to emergencies and one day it might be one of them that needs me.'

Mak followed her out of the room.

Helicopter mustering? Had the helicopter crashed?

He asked this as he caught up with her and was handed the car keys.

'It's more a gyrocopter,' she said. 'A small, light one-seater. Often home-made, which makes them, in my opinion, far more likely to come crashing down out of the sky. Unfortunately he's been working behind a herd of bullocks coming into town for the cattle sales so there's no nearby airstrip. The fellows with him don't think he's too badly injured but know not to move him, so we'll go out and if we need the flying doctors we'll contact them from there. We take the road west then the turnoff is exactly twelve kilometres on the right—we should be able to see them from there.'

Neena hoped the explanation and directions covered everything her colleague would need to know, as she'd just as soon not have him asking questions. For some reason the timbre of his voice and the intonation of his phrases had lingered in her head and made sleep difficult all night. Bad enough his image was imprinted on her eyelids so she couldn't avoid checking it out from time to time, but to have his voice whispering in her ears—that was too much!

But no worse than having him sitting beside her in the close confines of the car. He drove smoothly and efficiently—as he did everything, she suspected—but though she tried to concentrate on the delicious sandwiches Keira had supplied, her body was so aware of Mak's she felt embarrassed about it.

It had to be something to do with her hormones being out of kilter with the pregnancy. Maybe they were working overtime, and that was causing the way her skin was thirsting for a touch.

She gulped down some water, unable to believe where her mind had travelled.

Skin thirsting for his touch, indeed!

She must have read that somewhere.

And given the revelations of the previous evening, he was the last man in the world with whom she should get involved.

'We'll see them from here?' her tormentor asked as he turned onto the gravel road as directed.

'Check out that cloud of dust in the distance. They'll keep the mob moving and as they're coming down this road—and along the verges beside it—we'll have to drive through them.'

She paused and studied him for a moment,

although she didn't need to look at him to remember just how good-looking he was.

Or why he was really here!

'You have to drive very slowly through the herd, and some will nudge against you, but the men will have dogs and bikes and will help all they can.'

He turned towards her, frowning now.

'We drive through a mob of cattle, nudging some of them? What happens if we kill one?'

She had to laugh.

'If we do happen to have a fatal accident with one, then we could cut it up for meat.'

He glanced her way again.

'You're joking, right?'

'Not necessarily,' she said, still smiling. 'They're good fat bullocks on the way to market—someone would certainly cut it up for meat. See, here they come.'

She pointed ahead and Mak saw the cloud of dust she'd mentioned hazing the blue sky, but in front of it, like a red-brown river in flood, moving inexorably across the land, came the herd of red cattle, the stream as wide as the road and verges, maybe a hundred metres across, moving slowly, slowly, slowly, but gaining on them every second.

'Slow!' Neena reminded him, not that he'd needed reminding. The beasts were looking bigger by the moment and the thought of driving through them was challenging, to say the least.

A dusty cowboy on a motorbike pulled up beside the car and Mak let down the window.

'We left Tom where he fell. He's in shade and got water, about a kilometre behind us now.'

Neena seemed to think this was not unusual information, thanking the man and telling him she'd be in touch when she'd seen the patient.

'You okay to drive through?' the man asked Mak.

'I reckon so,' he said, then wondered if he'd already been in Wymaralong too long, 'reckon' being one of Ned's favourite words.

The cowboy rode off, taking a wide arc around the cattle, and Mak moved the vehicle forward, surprised at how little fuss the cattle made as he drew closer. Most moved sideways so a pathway was opened up, although every now and then one beast refused to give way and they had to wait for it to move, or try to edge around it.

'They're worked with bikes and vehicles these days so they don't object to them,' Neena said, while Mak looked around in wonder. It seemed to him they'd reached the middle of the herd, for as far as he could see in all directions were slowly moving cattle.

'I should have brought my camera,' he said to Neena, who smiled at him with the warm delight that made things buzz inside him.

'You won't forget it,' she said. 'It's the kind of image that stays in your mind for ever.'

'Like last night's sunset,' Mak said, then regretted it as the smile faded. She was obviously remembering the conversation that had preceded the sunset, and remembering he was—in her opinion—the enemy. But apart from being at least fifty per cent responsible for the pregnancy, what else did she hold against Theo and by extension his family? Had he made promises to her?

Hurt her so badly she couldn't forgive?

But would she have kept the baby, in that case?

Mak knew no matter how much thought he gave these questions, he wouldn't come up with answers. One day, perhaps, he could ask her—after all, she'd been totally blunt with him…

'Ah, nearly through,' she said. 'Now a kilometre or so. Drive fairly slowly—he might be in a paddock off the road. I'll keep an eye out this side, you watch the other.'

'Looking for a man lying in the shade of a tree?'

'Looking for a man and a machine that should retain at least some resemblance to a very small helicopter.'

'Got him!' Mak said, only minutes later, pulling the car off the road and into the meagre shade of a gum tree. The strange machine was in the shade of the single tree in a bare paddock on his side. He looked along the fence-line for a gate.

'We'll climb through, have a look at him, then if we have to drive closer, we'll cut the fence. Nick will have transferred the wire and fence strainers from my car to this one.'

Mak had no idea what fence strainers were but he was reasonably sure no women he had ever known would know, either—let alone be able to use them. More education lay ahead, he could see that.

At least he knew about barbed-wire fences and getting through them. He put his foot on the lowest wire and lifted the next one as high as he could to allow Neena to first throw her bag through then to clamber through herself. She turned to do the same for him, but things were never as easy as they looked and his shirt caught on a barb, and she had to lean over and free it, the faint scent of her body permeating his senses and stirring his libido.

This had to stop!

He picked up the bag and strode towards their patient, who was looking remarkably cheerful.

'Think I've done me knee again,' he said to Neena. 'M'back's okay and m'spine because I can wiggle my toes and move my fingers and my neck doesn't hurt, but the darned thing came down so quickly I put out my foot without thinking and jarred m'whole leg.'

Neena shook her head—what else could you do with an accident-prone cowboy?

'Tom, this is Mak, Mak, Tom. Tom badly damaged his knee about twelve months ago, coming off a quad bike. He went to Brisbane where the surgeons put it back together again far better than any of us expected, but believe me, they're not going to be pleased to see you again, Tom.'

Mak was examining the injured joint, poking and probing, his long fingers pressing against the swelling, his eyes on Tom's face as he looked for any signs of discomfort.

'I think it might be nothing more than a bad sprain,' Mak said. 'But we'll need to X-ray it to be sure. In fact, an ultrasound would be even better. Do you have an ultrasound machine?'

'We do, indeed,' Neena told him. 'Now! In fact, it was a donation from Hellenic Enterprises. Some bloke came out a while back and asked what we needed and came up with the ultrasound.'

Her voice trailed away and Mak guessed she was second-guessing this so timely donation. Seeing it now as a bribe?

Which it could well have been, but it did explain the amount on Con's expense sheet, and it would be invaluable today.

'Then do we get him into the car and take him back to town?' Mak asked, avoiding the subject of the ultrasound.

'After you've checked the rest of him over. Would you do that while I bring the car through? There's a cervical collar in my bag, whack that on him just in case.'

Neena was glad to get away, even if escape from

Mak's presence was only temporary. She'd had to touch his body as she'd unhooked his shirt and all the attraction stuff that she'd first felt with Theo had come back—only worse—and if falling for Theo had been a big mistake then falling for his uncle would be even more disastrous.

She looked along the fence-line, hoping to see a gate, but as there was no sign of one and she knew the paddock ran for kilometres, it was going to be a cutting job. Cutting the fence was the easy part—the strands of barbed wire springing away so she didn't have to move them out of the way of the car to drive through without damage to what paintwork it sported.

Mak had bound the wounded knee and splinted it with a stick—instinctive medicine or a bushie in the making?

'We'll lift him between us,' she suggested, moving to Tom's side.

'I don't think so,' Mak said, then he bent and easily lifted the lanky cowboy in his arms. 'You open the back door.'

Unused to being given orders, Neena hesitated, but only for a second—Tom must be getting heavier and heavier in Mak's arms.

He did allow her to help settle their patient so his legs were stretched along the seat.

'We'll drive back to the road then fix the fence,' she told Tom. 'See if you can fit the seat belt around you somehow while we're doing it.'

'We're doing it?' Mak said.

'It's easier with two,' she said, and grinned to herself—back in control. He'd know *nothing* about fixing fences!

She stopped just beyond the fence and got out her small roll of wire, two pairs of thick leather gloves, pliers and the handy fence strainer.

'May I ask why you carry all this gear? I can understand the gun I saw in there—no doubt it's to put injured animals out of their misery—but fence-fixing equipment?'

Neena was already twisting a length of her wire to one side of the severed barbed wire.

'It might take an hour to drive to the homestead and then another hour to get back to where Tom was, if we followed roads and tracks and went through gates. They run to huge paddocks out here, so sometimes it's just much quicker to go through the fences rather than around. But leave a fence down in this country and some other person with a rifle in the back of his or her car might shoot you.'

Mak, gloved and ready, started on the lowest strand of wire, using a second pair of pliers to attach a new piece, but his mind was more on his companion than on twisting wire. The more he saw of this woman, the more impressed he was, and he didn't want to be impressed by her. He didn't want to feel anything for her, or even get to know her better.

Yes you do!

The voice in his head was so loud he looked around, thinking maybe Neena had said the words as part of a conversation he'd missed. But she had fitted some contraption to the top wire, and was ratcheting the two ends of the fence towards each other, her lips were pressed tightly together while a small frown of concentration furrowed her brow.

'Let me do that,' Mak said, standing up and reaching out to take the handle from her.

'No, you twist the ends,' she told him and he saw that the strainers had pulled the barbed wire close enough for him to twist the end to the new piece Neena had inserted. 'That needs strong hands.'

'Wonderful!' he said, when they'd repeated the process four times and now had the whole fence back together.

'Wonderful indeed,' Neena said, 'and although I'll let the property owner know about the mend so he can do a proper job, I'm betting our makeshift patching will still be here when this kid has grandkids.'

She patted her stomach in a gesture Mak hadn't seen before, and for some reason it moved him immeasurably. In fact, he wanted to give the bump a pat himself.

What *was* he thinking?

'Do you want me to drive?' he asked, wanting to distance himself from the emotion he'd felt.

Neena grinned at him.

'Want to show Tom how good you are at driving through cattle?' she teased, and more emotion roiled inside him. 'Go for it,' she said. 'I'll finish my lunch.'

Fortunately Tom took over the conversation, asking Mak about himself, then talking about his own life, working on the property next to the one where he'd grown up.

'And did you build the gyrocopter?' Mak

asked, not quite believing what Neena had been saying earlier.

'Yes, it's my third and all of them have crashed, but you get enough good bits left over to start again.'

'Why would you want to start again?' Mak asked, and Tom laughed.

'You get on a bike behind a mob of cattle and you'll understand,' he said. 'At least up in the air, even if it's only ten feet, you don't get half the dust. Besides, the girls all think it's cool that I'm a helicopter pilot.'

'Without a licence,' Neena reminded him.

'Don't need it for the ones I fly,' Tom retorted, 'but the girls don't know that.'

They'd reached the dust cloud of the slowly moving mob of cattle once again and as Mak realised that driving through them this way was a very different matter, he glanced towards Neena, who was smiling at him with such sheer delight he knew she'd been waiting for the truth to dawn.

'They have their backs to me,' he said, although he'd guessed that was the cause of her amusement.

'So you have to nudge them aside,' she told him. Fortunately, before he'd worked out how to nudge a four-hundred-kilogram beast with a two-tonne vehicle and not kill the animal, the cowboy on the motorbike appeared again by his window.

'I'll push through them, you follow,' he said, so Mak steered the car through the cattle, keeping close to the bike as it thrust its way through the herd.

'Was that some kind of test?' he asked Neena when they were once again on the main road into town.

She smiled at him.

'No, I really did want to eat my lunch, but if it had been a test then you'd have passed with top marks.' She turned to the patient in the back seat. 'He's done well for a townie, hasn't he, Tom?'

'Not bad. He here to stay?'

'No, just passing through,' Neena replied, and Mak felt a flutter of something that couldn't possibly be disappointment that she'd written off his presence so casually.

I could stay, he wanted to say, but that was ridiculous.

But if the company funded another doctor...

And what about your career? Your dedication to emergency medicine? Your teaching ambitions?

It must be the heat, although the vehicle was air-conditioned, but for some reason he kept having these arguments in his head—or had voices telling him things he really didn't want to know.

'Where to?' he asked as the faded Christmas decorations strung across the streets announced they'd reached town.

'How are you at working an ultrasound machine?' Neena asked, then before he could reply she added, 'Actually, if it's foreign territory for you because you've got radiologists who do it, we've nurses at the hospital trained to use it. I'd like you to drop me back at the surgery, then take Tom up to the hospital. If you drive around the side you'll see the emergency entrance and someone will bring out a wheelchair for him. If it's just a sprain we'll keep him here and do the RICE thing for twenty-four hours, but if it's more badly damaged, get the hospital to contact the flying doctors and we'll get rid of him.'

'Hoy! That's me you're talking about,' Tom complained. 'And what's this RICE thing?'

'I thought you'd have been injured enough times to know it,' Neena told him. 'Rest, ice, compression and elevation. We'll keep you in so the nurses can make sure you are resting and you are keeping it elevated and they'll ice it for twenty minutes every hour.'

'Well, that's okay, and if Mak thinks it's only sprained he's probably right.'

'Because he's a man?' Neena asked, and the warning note in her voice made Mak smile, though he hid it as he waited for Tom's reply.

'Well, he's probably had sprains himself,' Tom said, digging himself a deeper hole.

'Whereas girls never sprain things?' Neena's voice was quiet but Tom must have caught on.

'Oh, sorry—that was a sexist thing to say, wasn't it?' he said, reaching over to pat Neena on the shoulder. 'You know I didn't mean anything. Everyone knows you're as good as any man—Whoops, it's getting worse.'

He gave her shoulder a squeeze with the hand that Mak felt had already lingered too long on her person.

'Friends?' Tom said, and she turned and smiled at him.

'Always friends, Tom,' she said, patting the hand that still rested on her shoulder.

Mak pulled up outside the surgery and before

he had the car in park she was out the door. At least that meant she was out of Tom's reach! Now she leaned back in, bending so he could see a hint of a full cleavage in the V-neck of her T-shirt.

'You know how to get to the hospital?' she said to Mak.

'I can show him if he doesn't,' Tom reminded her, which was just as well, as Mak's mouth had gone dry and words were beyond him.

Reacting like that to a hint of cleavage?

She was pregnant—of course she'd have full breasts!

He drove off, thinking he'd drop Tom at the hospital then go and sit with Maisie in the orchid house until he'd got some sense back into his head.

And some control back over his body!

Not that he could. He had to do the ultrasound on Tom's knee then, without a radiologist in town, read the results and work out if it *was* just a sprain. Would Tom's faith in male doctors be completely shattered if the knee turned out to be broken?

And while that shouldn't matter at all, Mak found himself hoping he was right, and not only for Tom's sake…

* * *

Neena all but ran into the surgery, so relieved to be out of Mak's presence and away from the curious vibes his body caused in hers that she greeted her afternoon staff with wide smiles.

In contrast to her morning staff, her afternoon staff were practically babies. In fact, both of them had been delivered by the practice nurse who worked mornings, and although both were younger than Neena, they were both married with children, working afternoons while their mothers collected the kids from kindergarten and minded them until dinnertime.

'New man in town, huh, Neena?' Louise, the younger of the pair, greeted her.

'Good-looking one, from all accounts,' Lisa added, smiling knowingly at her boss.

'Okay, you two, I don't need the double act. Who's first?'

'Charlie Weeks,' Lisa told her. 'After you called me from the car, I phoned all the patients who were cancelled earlier and he was the first to come back. Some said it wasn't important and re-booked for tomorrow, so you've only got three to see.'

'Which is a pity,' Louise complained, 'as it

means we won't have to call in Dr Wonderful as back-up. Is he really here to see if we need another doctor?'

Neena picked up Charlie's file and nodded in reply.

'And if he decides we do, will he be the one who stays?' Lisa asked.

'Definitely not,' Neena replied. 'He's some hotshot ER doctor from the city, currently doing a master's degree. Can you imagine someone like that wanting to work out here?'

But as she spoke she felt a sadness deep inside her, which was ridiculous as she barely knew the man, and she certainly didn't need another man messing up her life. If she managed to get another doctor, she'd make sure it was a woman!

'Come on in, Charlie,' she said to her patient, and she led him into the examination room, her mind switching from trivia—for that's all it was—to work in an instant.

Or most of her mind! As she opened her emails to check on some blood-test results for Charlie she found the email from Hellenic Enterprises telling her that Mak was on his way…

'These internet messages aren't all they're cracked up to be, Charlie,' she said, while his blood-test results printed out. 'Supposedly it's instant information, but if there's a hitch in the system the information can come too late.'

'Too late for what, Neena?' Charlie asked, sounding extremely puzzled, as well he might have been.

'Too late for me to high-tail it out of town,' she said, then she showed him the test results, explained how his elevated PSI count was an indication of trouble with his prostate, but as it hadn't gone up any higher in the six months since the last test there was no need to worry about it.

'We talked about all this when you first found the trouble,' Charlie reminded her. 'And we decided, at eighty-four, even with the problem, I'd probably get another ten years and doing nothing meant the ten years would be good years, while having an operation and chemo with no guarantee of longer than ten years, I'd be sick and sorry for myself.'

He paused, then added, 'It's okay—it doesn't bother me, so don't you be worrying about it.'

Neena smiled. So many of her patients felt

they should be the ones comforting her, not the other way around.

'Hear you got yourself a young camel. I've got some good lucerne hay at the moment and I brought in a half bale for when he's ready to try something solid. I'd drop it at your place, but I've got to get back home and Ned always chats, so can I leave it here?'

'I'll come out and get it,' Neena said, as she finished examining the old man, noting down his pulse and blood pressure, aware as always most patients came in for a chat, but needing to keep records of their health all the same.

She walked out with Charlie, told him in no uncertain terms that she was quite capable of lifting a half bale of hay, and proceeded to do just that, tugging it up by the strings until it was resting on the sides of the utility before lifting it into her arms. She was sorry her car wasn't there so she could transfer the bale of hay straight into it. Charlie's ute was parked at the front of the car park and she'd just lifted the bale free when Mak drove in. Guessing the hay wasn't for the surgery, he pulled up beside her, leapt out and seized the bale from her hands.

'You're pregnant, woman, you shouldn't be lifting things.'

'I told her that,' Charlie chimed in, but Neena ignored both of them, simply opening the back of the big car so Mak could put the bale inside.

'What happened with Tom?' she asked Mak when she'd thanked Charlie and watched him drive off.

'Bad sprain but no sign of any ligament damage or disruption of the joint. I've left him there flirting with the nurses. Phyllis and Marnie are gone and Mr Temple told me you said he could go home today, but one of the nurses said he tries that with everyone and not to believe him. Is that right?'

The dark hazel eyes were fixed on her face and although this was very much a colleague-to-colleague conversation, Neena felt her insides heating up to rival the forty-plus temperature out there in the car park.

'He does,' she agreed, turning away from that steady regard. 'Let's get inside.'

But as he began to follow her into the cool of the surgery she realised her mistake, and turned back to face him.

'Actually, most of the patients have re-booked for tomorrow—I've one post-partum appointment and a triple antigen for a pre-schooler and that's it. You could go home.'

'Home's a long way off,' he reminded her with a smile that made her wish she'd kept walking. 'If it's okay with you, I'll come in and talk to the staff about how they've found having the extra people in town.'

'Louise and Lisa will *love* that,' Neena muttered, again heading for the front door.

So they'd flirt a little with him—so what? she told herself, but the cross feeling in her head and the tightness in her chest didn't go away until she'd finished for the day and driven home— alone, as Louise had driven Mak home—and headed for the stables to see Albert.

CHAPTER FIVE

IT WAS obviously fate that as she struggled through the door to drop the bale of hay in the feed shed, she'd catch sight of the man she was trying to avoid. He was leading Albert around the yard behind the stables, his arm around the small animal's neck, talking quietly to him, as if introducing him to the concept of fences and gates and yards.

'Ned said he hadn't had time to walk him today.'

'Monday—baking day,' Neena confirmed, feeling surprised Mak had taken on the job himself. 'You could as easily make the sun rise in the west as change Ned's housekeeping schedule.'

This is good, she congratulated herself. You're having an easy, normal conversation with the man. This is how it has to be. But as she moved closer to him, wanting to pet Albert and feel his rubbery lips in the palm of her hand, the zinging attraction stuff started up again and she excused herself and walked away, deciding a cold shower was better than the feel of rubbery lips against her palm.

Rubbery legs didn't help her escape…

Mak watched her go, wondering if her hasty departure meant she was upset with him for walking the little camel.

Surely not, although he was glad she was gone. Even with hay all over her T-shirt and bits clinging to her long plait, she was beautiful, and something about that beauty—the unexpectedness of it, or the sense of strength beneath the perfect features—affected him in a way he didn't want to think about.

But seeing her half an hour later, when Albert was back in his shed and Mak had taken the steps two at a time to reach the veranda to find her sitting on the western corner of it, drying her hair in the dying rays of the sun, made him realise that the attraction he felt for her wasn't something that not thinking about it would vanquish.

She had her back to him, so all he could see of her was the curtain of black hair and her hand as it rose and fell, brushing through the silken strands.

Silken strands—where *was* his mind?

Yet he knew that's how they'd feel—as soft as silk.

'Need a hand?'

The words came out without forethought and too late he wished them unsaid, for she'd spun around and was staring at him with an expression that bordered on fear. Or was he imagining that?

'Did you sneak up those steps?' she demanded. Not fear, maybe anger—but why would she be angry?

'I thundered up them,' he told her, moving closer and taking the brush from her nerveless fingers, in spite of the voices in his head warning him to stay right away from her—voices that made a lot of sense. 'Tip your head forward.'

Why had she let him take the brush?

Why was she tipping her head forward?

Neena had no answer to the questions, or the dozens of others her body was posing. All she knew was that sitting here on the corner of her own veranda, feeling the brush run down through her hair, was the most exciting moment of her life thus far.

And if that wasn't the most ridiculous thought she'd ever had, then she didn't know what was!

'Not good, is it?' the man wielding the brush said quietly in a voice that rasped its way past his lips.

And though she knew, she had to ask.

'What?' she whispered.

'The attraction between us. The attraction we both felt when we danced on Saturday night—remember?'

There, it was said—well, he'd said it but did she have to admit to it?

'You're not going to deny it, are you?' he continued, his voice still husky with the emotion she didn't want to acknowledge.

'At least I've got the excuse of my hormones being in a tangle because I'm pregnant,' Neena told him. 'And speaking of which, I don't see how you can possibly be attracted to a pregnant woman anyway.'

'A very beautiful pregnant woman,' he said, touching her head to tilt it to the other side. 'Although the fact that she's pregnant by my dead nephew does complicate matters somewhat.'

Neena pulled away, but not before a shiver went through her when he mentioned Theo. She reached around her head and caught the shining mass of hair between her hands, then with nimble fingers moving almost too quickly for him to follow she plaited her hair and slipped a band around the bottom of the pigtail, flinging it back over her shoulder.

She'd drawn away from him—not physically but mentally—folding in on herself, bringing up an almost tangible shield.

'You still love him?' Mak probed, taking the chair beside her, allowing her space but not too much.

She turned and stared at him, a frown between her brows.

'Why would you ask that?'

'Because if you do, then this attraction might feel wrong to you. As if you're letting down his memory or something. That would make you feel you have to fight it.'

'You're assuming the attraction,' she said, her voice stronger now, so Mak realised she was ready for a fight.

'I am,' he said. 'But I'm nearly forty years old—I've felt attraction before and I know darned well that one this strong is never one-sided. People talk about pheromones and give all kind of reasons for attraction, but as far as I'm concerned, what strengthens an initial interest and builds it into attraction is the response of the other person. In part, I agree it's probably chemical, but it has to be more than that. Something bred into us to ensure the continuation of the species, I imagine.'

Neena stared at him, then shook her head.

'I can't believe we're having this conversation.'

Mak smiled, which sent her heart into excited palpitations.

'It's not exactly a conversation as I'm doing all the talking, but it would help if you put in a bit now and then. Do you find it as inconvenient as I do? Should we agree to ignore it as much as possible, which seems to me the sensible thing to do, especially as neither of us really trusts the other?'

'Well, you're right about that—about the trust. You're the last man on earth I'd trust. So of course we're going to ignore it—that's if it exists at all. What else can we possibly do? Have an affair? As if I haven't made enough of a mess of my life already!'

Neena stood up and walked away, shaking her head, unable to think straight when Mak was sitting next to her, spouting all kinds of rubbish about attraction. He talked as if it was something you could turn on and off at will. She *wished*!

Although she *could* ignore it! Just pretend it didn't exist—that would be the best idea. She hadn't admitted she felt it—or had she?

Maybe she had!

She tried to replay the conversation in her head, but all she could remember was the feel of the brush running through her hair, guided by Mak's hands.

Mak's hands…

Don't go there! Her head screamed the warning and she knew she had to listen. Back in the sanctuary of her bedroom she shrugged off the light cotton robe she'd put on after her shower and clambered into shorts and a T-shirt. Even with the air-cooler working, it was hot enough to make her cheeks burn.

Although that could have been the hair-brushing thing…

Mak watched her walk away, the last rays of the sun shining through the light wrap she wore so he could see the slim lines of her body, the neat bulge of the baby, the full breasts…

A gentleman wouldn't be looking.

But a gentleman probably wouldn't have mentioned the attraction, either. Just because she'd been honest with him about her feelings towards his family, it didn't mean she'd want him being honest about *his* feelings.

Not that attraction had anything to do with feelings. As he'd said—it was a chemical thing. And as *she'd* quite rightly pointed out, there wasn't a thing they could do about it. Talk about living in a fishbowl!

And for the first time it occurred to him just how hard her decision to go ahead with this pregnancy must have been, the doctor in a small country town suddenly joining the ranks of unmarried mothers. No matter how much people loved her, there'd have been criticism and snide remarks and quite a lot, he imagined, of disapproval.

Yet she'd gone ahead with it, which brought him back to whether or not it had been a deliberate act, as he'd first suspected!

Although she'd sounded regretful when she'd talked about the mess she'd made of her life…

Was it the heat making it too hard for him to think straight?

Or the attraction?

He'd have a shower.

A cold shower.

And not entirely because the temperature out here was hot enough to melt the fillings in his teeth…

They were sitting down to what, according to Neena, was Ned's Monday night special—home-made meat pies—when the phone call came.

'I'll keep them hot,' Ned said, whisking the plates off the table before Mak could take a mouthful.

'But it mightn't be a callout,' he protested, his taste buds in revolt over the denial of the tanta-lising meal.

'It will be,' Ned said, shaking his head at Mak's naiveté.

Neena appeared at that moment, sticking her head into the kitchen.

'Come on, Dr First Response, you can tell me what to do with this situation.'

He followed her out of the house and down the front steps.

'Where to?' he asked.

'A property about forty kilometres out of town. The flying doctor's on the way. They'll land on the property, our job is to stabilise the guy.'

'Can't the ambulance attendants do that? Does it always have to be you?'

'It does when the ambulance is out of town the other way, taking a woman in labour to Baranock.'

'Maybe next time someone gives the town money they should get a second ambulance,' Mak grumbled, his mind still on the dinner he was missing.

Or was it being back in the car with Neena that was making him cranky? In the confines of the car all the chemistry she was able to deny or ignore seemed to be stronger.

'What's the problem?' he asked, thinking work talk would be a good diversion from food and pheromones.

'Guy nailed his foot to the floor.'

'You *have* to be joking!'

She turned towards him and grinned.

'Why ever would you think that? You must get nail-gun accidents at your ER.'

Light dawned and Mak had to admit that they did get regular nail-gain accidents showing up.

'But that's not the point,' he said. 'Think about it. I've been here two days and we're had burns victims—okay, they are fairly common—

rescued a baby camel, treated a guy from a gyrocopter crash and now we're heading out to a bloke who's nailed his foot to the floor. I know diversity makes medicine more interesting, but this much?'

Neena laughed. He sounded so put out by it all.

'Isn't variety the spice of life?' she teased.

'Maybe, but there's another cliché that fits—the one about having too much of a good thing,' he muttered, so grumpy she wondered what was really upsetting him.

'Is it missing your dinner making you so tetchy?'

She glanced his way as she asked the question and saw his frown.

'Men don't do tetchy!' he told her, but there was no further elaboration, although his frown stayed firmly in place.

Given the conversation they'd had earlier—or he'd had earlier—perhaps it was better not to ask what was upsetting him. So instead she talked about the country through which they were driving, explaining that originally it had all been sheep grazing land, although now more and more farmers were going into cattle.

'And what do the animals eat?' her non-tetchy

companion demanded, looking out at the landscape lit now by a nearly full moon. 'Stones?'

Neena laughed again.

'It does look barren, but the little bushes and dried clumps of grass contain good nutrients for sheep or cattle, and after rain or when flood waters wash through this country, it comes alive again, green and lush.'

'I find that very hard to believe,' Mak said, but his voice sounded more relaxed and he was peering with more interest at the country through which they passed.

Finally she pulled across a grid into the property they were visiting.

'Why would someone have been using a nail-gun at this time of the evening?' Mak asked.

'I didn't ask so I can only guess, but I'd say he finished his real work for the day—the outdoor stuff—then decided to get on with his renovations. The property owner is Wilf Harris. He's only recently married, and his and his wife's families are coming to stay for Christmas so he decided to enclose his veranda to make some more room for the influx.'

'And he just happened to have a nail-gun?'

'He probably borrowed it,' Neena said, as the lights of the homestead appeared in the distance.

'And used it with no proper training in its use,' Mak muttered, and Neena realised he was tetchy again.

She said nothing, hoping he'd get over whatever was upsetting him before they met up with the Harrises.

Megan was waiting on the front veranda and she raced towards the car as Neena pulled up.

'I kept him warm but he said not to touch his foot so I didn't, although I gave him a chair to sit on,' she said, the panicky words tumbling over each other as they came rushing out.

'That's fine,' Neena assured her. 'And this is Dr Stavrou. He's a city doctor so he sees a lot of nail-gun accidents.'

Megan turned to Mak as if he were an angel sent from heaven.

'Oh, thank you so much for coming,' she said, throwing her arms around him and giving him a hug. 'He's round here.'

She led the way around the veranda to the back corner where her husband sat, wrapped in a blanket as she'd said, his face ashen with pain.

'I didn't want to make it bleed more by taking it out,' he said.

'What have you had for the pain?' Neena asked, knowing the flying doctor's medical chest that every property had would contain morphine.

'Only a couple of paracetamol. Megan's new to the bush and I didn't want to pass out from the morphine and leave her on her own.'

Neena heard Mak's grunt of disbelief, but he was already kneeling at Wilf's feet, examining the injury.

'I think a saw—a hacksaw—to detach it from the flooring,' he suggested, standing up and turning to Megan, asking her to show him where Wilf kept his tools.

'On the wall in the shed,' Wilf told her, and she led Mak away.

Neena checked her patient, taking his pulse and blood pressure, but thinking how easily Mak seemed to be fitting into country medicine, although his patients usually came to him with their accidents, so he didn't have to deal with them in situ. She found some local anaesthetic in her bag, and concentrated on her patient.

'I'm going to try to deaden all around the wound so you won't feel it while we cut you free,' she told him. 'Did the flying doctors give you an ETA?'

'Depends on a delivery they're doing,' Wilf told her. 'But the latest will be in two hours.'

What could happen in another two hours? The nail had already been in there for an hour. It would have oil on it but be relatively clean and while it was there, it was plugging any holes it had made in veins or arteries. But was it also stopping blood getting to Wilf's toes?

They wouldn't know until they got his shoe off and to do that they'd have to remove the nail.

Mak was back, although she didn't want to ask him his opinion of the best option as a first response person in front of Wilf and Megan. They might be concerned to hear people they trusted with their lives debating options.

'I've deadened the area around the wound,' she told Mak, who squatted beside her, the hacksaw in his hand.

'You right, mate?' he asked, looking up at Wilf.

'Go for it,' Wilf said, but rather than watch what Mak was doing he turned away, and Megan wrapped her arms around him so his face was hidden against her chest.

The screeching of the hacksaw set Neena's teeth on edge, but she sat on the floor across from Mak and held Wilf's foot as still as she could.

'Okay, you're free,' Mak said, within minutes that had only seemed like hours. 'Stay where you are for the moment. Neena, I'll show you where the hacksaw goes in case you ever need it.'

Neena followed him off the veranda, aware he'd been thinking the same thing she had— wanting to discuss the next move but not in front of Megan and Wilf.

'What's your opinion on leaving it in?' he asked as they reached the bottom of the steps.

'I'm dithering,' Neena told him. 'I can't decide, although I think when you take into consideration the golden rule of "first do no harm" then leaving it in is probably the best option. If we reef it out we could do more damage and cause more bleeding. What worries me is whether leaving it in might compromise the eventual use of his foot in some way.'

'I don't see that it can,' Mak told her. 'When's the flying doctor due?'

'Original ETA was within two hours, so I'd say he's getting close now, and it's three quarters of an hour's flight to their base so they could have him in an operating theatre within a couple of hours.'

'Then we leave it in,' Mak said as they walked into the shed, then suddenly he flung the hacksaw onto the ground, seized Neena in his arms and whipped her off the ground, racing out into the hot night air.

'Put me down!' she shrieked, kicking at him. 'What on earth got into you?'

'Snake,' he said, clinging even more tightly to her, hurrying back towards the house.

'What kind of snake?' Neena demanded, still wriggling, although there was something very exciting about being held in Mak's arms.

'I didn't wait to ask it,' Mak said, fairly breathless now, as Neena was no lightweight for all her slight build.

'It was Stanley,' Wilf said from the veranda, smiling as if he'd enjoyed the little drama that had played out in front of his eyes. 'Harmless old carpet snake that's lived in the shed for years. He keeps the rats and mice down.'

Mak dropped his burden, slightly put out that his

heroic act had been for nothing—although holding Neena in his arms had definitely been a bonus.

'You didn't need to tell her that,' he complained to Wilf. 'I might have made some points for saving her life.'

'You'd need to do more than rescue her from a snake to catch our Neena,' Wilf said. 'Especially now!'

'Will you two stop talking about me?' Neena ordered. 'Megan, are the landing strip lights on?'

'No, I'll go and turn them on,' Megan said, and disappeared into the house.

'It's good having the lights.' Mak had walked over to Wilf and had casually picked up his wrist to check his pulse, Wilf explaining a new aspect of country life to Mak while he stood there. 'Before we got them we had to take vehicles out to light the strip and guide the planes in, or light fires, but now the strip is lit all the way down. Got solar panels out there that provide the power for the lights. Been a great thing, the solar, out here in the bush.'

Neena had remained at the top of the steps, carefully out of range of Mak's physical presence, although she was beginning to believe that Mars might be too close…

She watched him talking to Wilf, quietly checking their patient over with a minimum of fuss, and an ache started up in her heart, as if the month was already over and he was gone.

No, this couldn't be. Just because he'd talked about attraction—and because he'd danced with her and held her in his arms…

The plane swooping overheard diverted her.

'Mak and I will carry you down to the car and drive you out to the airstrip,' she said to Wilf. 'Have you talked to Megan about whether she wants to stay here or follow you to town?'

'I don't want her staying here on her own,' Wilf said, 'but there're the chooks and the lamb to be fed tomorrow and my mum and dad are down at the coast for a few weeks' holiday.'

'I'll get someone to come out and feed the animals,' Neena offered. 'Actually, Ned can come out and stay here until you get back.'

The words were no sooner out of her mouth than she realised what that would mean—that she'd be alone in the house with Mak. Not that being alone with him would matter. She'd already decided that the only way to tackle the attraction was to ignore it, and she could do that just as easily without Ned.

She'd walked across to where Wilf was still seated but hadn't bargained for Mak's obstinacy.

'You drive down to the airstrip and get someone from the plane to help me lift Wilf,' he said.

'But I can take one side,' Neena argued.

'No way!' both men chorused, Mak adding, 'and don't suggest Megan help. Just for once in your life do as you're told and go and get help!'

Neena gave him one of her best glares but she did turn away, only to find a vehicle already driving towards them. Megan had met the plane.

They saw Wilf safely dispatched, then waited while Megan tidied the house and packed a bag, eventually following her into town where she'd arranged to pick up her mother for the three-hour drive to the hospital where Wilf would be treated.

'Will Ned mind you offering his services?' Mak asked when he was once again a passenger in Neena's car, heading back to town.

'No, he loves the chance to get back out into the bush. He lived in the country most of his life, working on properties, droving cattle and sheep, breaking in horses. A man of many talents.'

'Including cooking, and taking care of people's clothes—that doesn't seem to fit.'

Neena turned and smiled at her passenger.

'Most outback men are self-sufficient, and at one stage Ned was cook for a gang of shearers and there's no one more fussy about their food than shearers. He cooked at the hospital, too, for a while.'

'Until you got him,' Mak said, and Neena shook her head.

'No, he got me,' she said softly. 'Without Ned I'd never have made it to where I am today—never have got through high school, let alone through university.'

She sounded so sad Mak longed to ask her for an explanation, but he sensed she'd erected a barrier between them and he didn't know her well enough to break it down. Didn't know her well enough to be feeling all the things he felt, either, if it came to that!

He hid a sigh—he seemed to be forever sighing these days—sighing or shaking his head.

Neena had been doing okay in the 'ignoring the attraction' stakes until he'd lifted her into his arms, and suddenly, from being a woman to whom self-sufficiency was practically a religion, she'd turned into a weak and feeble female who

wanted nothing more than to be held and protected and fussed over for the rest of her life.

Preferably in Mak's arms.

Which was a very scary thought.

She turned her mind to medical matters.

'If Wilf had turned up in your ER, would you
have removed the nail or sent him to Theatre for
surgeons to do it?'

'I'd send him to Theatre every time,' Mak
replied. 'In ER we'd have X-rayed the foot to see
the exact position of the nail, then, if all the
theatres were busy, I might have removed it. By
sending him to Theatre, surgeons can do any repair
work to nerves, ligaments and bones while they
have his foot opened up, whereas removing it
would only have been a temporary measure until
we could get an orthopaedic surgeon involved.'

'So as first response we did the right thing.'

'There's no real right thing,' Mak told her, 'just
what seems best at the time.'

'Then what exactly is your master's thesis
about?'

'It's more about how we can teach lay people
to react when someone close to them is in trouble.
Which advertising proves the most effective?

How much information is enough—how much too much? You know the FAST campaign?'

'For stroke victims?' Neena queried. 'Facial weakness, arm weakness, speech difficulty, time to act fast.'

'That's the one,' Mak said. 'Every home in Australia has been given one of the little FAST cards and should have it stuck on their fridge, showing them how to test a person they suspect might be having a stroke. If we can educate the public enough that we get response teams to the patient as soon as possible, we can give the victim drugs which can nullify the effect of the stroke before too much damage has been done.'

'But won't having dozens of little cards stuck on the fridge only confuse people?'

Mak's chuckle slithered beneath her skin and started all the responses she was trying so hard not to feel.

'That's one of the things I'm looking at—just how much do people need to know and how much is too much.'

She pulled into her parking spot at the bottom of the steps and climbed hastily out of the car.

'I'll just check on Albert before I come in.

Ned will have heard the car and will be heating your dinner.'

Don't come with me, in other words, Mak thought to himself, but being separated from Neena, if only for a short time, wasn't such a bad idea right now. He could still feel the weight of her body in his arms and was carrying the scent of her in his nostrils.

How could he feel such a strong attraction to a woman he didn't entirely trust? And why the attraction, anyway? Hadn't he learned to avoid that? Learned to enjoy relationships that had no ties beyond the physical?

Although attraction was physical…

The idea that this attraction was more than that startled him so much he stopped on the veranda and looked out at the town, trying to work out what was going on, not only in his body but inside his head. The more he saw of Neena— with patients, with Maisie, with the camel—the more he found himself admiring her—and the harder it was to consider she might be the con- niving female of his original suspicions.

He swallowed the sigh that nearly came out and headed for his late dinner.

'She out with that camel?' Ned asked as Mak entered the kitchen.

'Just checking on him, she says,' Mak responded.

'While I have to keep her dinner hot,' Ned complained, but he didn't sound too put out about it.

He got me, Neena had said, but although Mak longed to ask the older man to explain this cryptic comment, he didn't feel he could, so he ate his dinner—delicious—then on Ned's suggestion took his coffee through to the living room, intending to turn on the television. But once there, the photos on the piano drew him closer and he sipped his coffee and studied them.

A little girl with two pigtails and no front teeth was photographed in front of the steps of the old house. She was clutching a hamster in her hands and beaming with the pride of ownership. Another photo showed a very beautiful Indian woman, younger than Neena but not her. Her mother? Yes, there she was again with a short, turbaned man, love shining from both their faces. Photos of the couple with a baby, the baby growing, then no photos for a long time until one of Neena in her graduation robes, a man beside her smiling proudly—and though he was younger, the photo was unmistakably one of Ned.

Looking at it more closely, Mak picked out a crowd of people, not anonymous others at the graduation but Wymaralong locals—there was Maisie, on sticks, not in a wheelchair, and Lauren from the hospital, and the old receptionist and even older surgery nurse. Mak felt emotion stir inside him. She may have been an orphan but she'd never been alone—neither had she ever been unloved, for all the faces in the background beamed with the same pride as Ned's.

So what must they all be thinking of the pregnancy?

Weren't country people more likely to be shocked by an unmarried mother having a baby?

And did the whole town know the story of it that Marnie and Phyllis had talked of? The Rat— indubitably Theo...

Mak almost shook his head, but as he'd told himself he wasn't going to do that any more, he didn't, simply going back to the early photos of Neena, lifting them and studying them, wondering if the baby would grow into a little girl with two pigtails and no front teeth.

A little girl would be nice, he was thinking, when he caught up with his straying mind and hauled it back under control. Neither Neena nor her baby were any concern of his—except for where the baby's life would have an impact on his family, and his own determination to be involved in all plans for the baby's future.

Family!

Family Neena wanted nothing to do with.

He heard her in the kitchen, talking to Ned, no doubt explaining about the accident and speaking to him about going out to Wilf and Megan's house.

'I hope you can cook,' he heard her say, and turned to see her coming into the living room, a cup of something—probably not coffee or tea—in her hand.

'Hot chocolate, my least favourite drink but it's better than nothing,' she said, catching his quick glance at the cup. 'And don't think just because Ned is leaving, you can take over as the caffeine police—I am very aware I have to limit myself. I have one cup of coffee—weak—a day and that is it!'

'I can cook,' Mak told her, wondering if this

conversation was in some way a truce between them. 'But I doubt I can mix camel milk formula.'

Neena smiled at him.

'That I can manage,' she said. 'And you needn't cook every night, we can eat at the hospital or the café or the pub. Breakfast you can help yourself. There's always cereal and yoghurt and bread for toast.'

'You don't do cooked breakfasts?' Mak teased, and won another smile.

'I'm the world's worst cook,' she admitted. 'Maisie felt I should know how and she tried to teach me, but I get distracted and things get burnt. She took to stocking the freezer with bread and the pantry with tins of baked beans and packets of instant soup mix so if she did have to go away I wouldn't starve to death.'

'And if you have a daughter, will you get Ned to teach her?'

Had he broken the moment of rapport that Neena paused before answering? But then she smiled again—three smiles in one evening.

'I'll get Ned to teach him or her, boy or girl— why discriminate? Your mother obviously didn't!'

'No, for all she is a very traditional Greek, she

made sure both her children not only learned to cook but knew how to work the washing machine and turn on an iron. She was proud when my sister decided to study engineering. I sometimes wondered if perhaps she'd have liked to have had the chance to take up a career herself.'

'Is is too late now?' Neena asked, and Mak, although he'd sworn he wasn't going to shake his head again, found it moving from side to side.

'Of course it isn't,' he said, smiling at the woman whose simple question had provided a possible solution to something that had been concerning him since his father's death—how to shake his mother out of her unhappiness. 'Anthropology—that's always interested her. She needn't do a whole degree but she can begin some study, maybe go along on some digs.'

He moved towards Neena, removed the cup from her hands, set it down, and swung her into his arms, whirling her around and around.

'You are a genius!'

And then, because she was in his arms, as he set her back on her feet, he kissed her.

CHAPTER SIX

IT WAS a friendly kiss, a thank-you kiss, nothing more, Neena tried to tell herself, but as his lips firmed against hers and her body, bulky stomach and all, pressed tightly against his, the embers of desire she had been sure she could control flared into life, heating her body to meltdown.

This from a kiss?

She had to break away—move—put space between them, yet her body refused to obey her brain's commands, staying clasped against Mak's chest, her lips now responding to the kiss, her tongue tangling with his, her heart beating so erratically she could feel its pounding right through her body.

Or was it his heart pounding?

No, hers, for she could hear the thunder of it in her ears, all senses on alert.

All for a kiss…

Mak broke the spell, which was just as well as Neena doubted she could have moved to save herself. He put his hands on her shoulders and eased away from her, then he moved her back towards a chair, sat her down, and returned her cup of chocolate to her hand.

'Well, that was interesting,' he said, as if he'd successfully completed some kind of experiment. He sat down across from her and put his feet up on a footstool, looking as relaxed and at ease as Neena's father had, when he'd finished dinner and had been relaxing in the living room while she'd played the piano.

She actually glanced towards the piano, wondering if she'd see the ghost of her younger self sitting there.

But the tall man sitting in her living room was a very different proposition from her gentle father. The tall man sitting there wanted control over her child—she had to remember that. Theo had seduced her for one reason—the challenge—and this man was doing it for another—she had to remember that, too.

'I was a thirty-four-year-old virgin, I wasn't

that hard to seduce, especially not for someone like Theo.'

She had no idea why she'd felt impelled to pass on that information except, perhaps, in case the kiss had given Mak ideas, she needed to let him know she'd fallen for one Greek recently but wasn't going to do it again.

'A thirty-four-year-old virgin?'

'You don't have to make it sound like an extinct animal!' she grumbled, not at all sure why she was having his conversation but now it had started wanting to get it over and done with.

He smiled at her, which was something she wished he wouldn't do.

'I thought they *were* extinct,' he said.

'I'd put them more in the rare category, and so coming under the protected species act—or protection of some kind, which was my situation.'

'As in?' he prompted, and this time it was Neena who sighed.

'I know you haven't been here long, but you've met some of the people of the town.' She walked across to the piano and picked up the graduation photograph, handing it to him. 'Look at them. They're just the ones who came to Brisbane for the ceremony. The whole town helped send me to uni, they fundraised to pay my higher education fees and boarding costs. But I had to work for spending money, and I wasn't a genius so I had to study in virtually all my spare time. Yes, there were boys there, male students, and some I really liked, but—'

'But no time for an affair?' Mak prompted, still looking at the photo.

'When all those people had faith in me? When all they wanted was for me to graduate and come back to them so the town had a doctor again? What if I'd fallen in love with someone in the city? One of those young men? Someone who wouldn't live in the country? Couldn't live in the country? I'd have been letting all the townspeople down, I couldn't have lived with myself.'

Mak shook his head.

'That was some burden of obligation you took on,' he murmured, but as Neena retrieved the photo, *she* shook her head, smiling as she did so.

'Not really,' she said, her forefinger touching the faces in the photo, her smile serene. 'They all loved me, you see. You talk about your family and what they mean to you—well, these people are my family so it was no sacrifice at all.'

'And Theo?'

That story was too tawdry to tell, so Neena shook her head, already regretting sharing even this small part of her life with this man.

'I'd like to know,' he said, his voice deep and husky as if he really meant the interest he was showing.

The timbre of the words shivered across her skin, reminding her just how dangerous he was, while the unspoken memory of the kiss lingered in the room like a large, unwanted ghost.

'I'm sure you would,' she said, putting on a smile so he wouldn't guess how his voice—and the ghost—was affecting her. How his *presence* was affecting her! 'But a girl can only handle so much true confession in one night. Now I'm off to bed. The last few days have been a bit hectic and a good night's sleep's in order.'

She stood up and though she'd intended leaving the room, she noticed the photos on the piano were out of order and moved across to straighten them.

'Do you play?' he asked, as she hovered by the instrument.

'Yes,' she said, lifting the lid and tapping out a few notes from a tune her father had loved.

'Play for me?'

Mak's voice was husky again but this time instead of slithering over her skin it went straight to her knees, which weakened so she had to sit down on the piano stool, her hands spreading across the keys, the notes of the sad love song filling the room.

'Is it Theo you're remembering?' Mak asked, coming to stand behind her as she sat on the stool, her head bowed over the yellowed keys.

'Never!' she told him, strength returning with the denial, enough strength to shut the lid of the piano and stand up so she could escape Mak's presence. 'Apart from the baby, I have no good memories of Theo.'

'Yet you kept his child? It *is* his child?'

'Would he otherwise have left it something?' she said, looking into the hazel eyes, daring him to repeat the question she'd ignored.

He took the dare.

'Why?'

Was it a night for confession? Was it something to do with the moon and stars being in some celestial conjunction that she felt a need to tell someone why she'd made a decision she knew the whole town wondered about? Although maybe the town didn't wonder? Maybe they assumed it was because she'd loved Theo, rat that he had been!

'The baby wasn't to blame for what had happened and I suppose, if you go right back to the beginning, it was because I *had* been a thirty-four-year-old virgin! My marriage prospects weren't all that bright. All the young men in town had been snapped up while I'd been at university, and I don't know that I'd have fallen in love with any of them if they had been available. The pregnancy was an accident yet when I realised I *was* pregnant, it seemed as if it was meant to be.'

She moved away from Mak's too intense scrutiny because she didn't want him seeing the emotion that was stirred up in her body.

'The baby would be family,' she said quietly. '*My* family! I know that is totally selfish but I haven't had a family for a long time…'

And on that note she escaped, heading for her bedroom, her insides churning so badly she thought she might be sick.

Was it *all* about family? Mak wondered when

she'd departed so precipitously. His family—her family!

Shouldn't it be about the baby?

He found he had no answer to that or any of the other questions so he, too, went to bed, where sleep took a long time to come, the memory of Neena's lips on his, her body pressed against him, caused him so much physical discomfort he eventually got up and showered again, telling himself the trip out to the Harrises' property had left him hot and dusty.

Neena heard the water running in the shower and couldn't help but wonder what he looked like naked—imagining him, skin slicked with water, standing under the cooling jets. Her knowledge of anatomy and her experience with naked male patients meant that the masculine body held no secrets for her—she'd seen them all, fat and thin, big and small, but Mak's body would be something else! Taut and trim, the muscles beneath the skin—and she knew they were there from the effortless way he'd lifted and carried her—beautifully defined.

And imagining, her own body grew hot and she felt the fever of desire flooding through her veins.

Damn it all! Hadn't she learned her lesson from Theo—hadn't one lot of fever given her immunity from a recurrence?

Although the Theo fever had been purely physical and, as it had turned out, very transient. Mak fever was different. She'd known that as soon as she'd met the man. Mak wasn't anything like the charming, conceited, spoiled young man his nephew had been.

Or was he?

Who was she to judge?

Hadn't her judgement been proven wrong a couple of times before?

She felt her cheeks heat against the pillow as she remembered the youthful indiscretions that had brought Ned into her life, the night he'd caught her in the back seat of a car with the wildest teenager in town…

Why is it we remember the bad things—the things we feel guilty about? she wondered for the hundredth time. She could remember Ned's voice, his anger, as clearly as if it was yesterday, yet couldn't remember her mother's voice.

Damn it all, she thought again, sitting up this time, readjusting the sheet which was the only covering the hot night allowed. I have to think happy thoughts, not gloomy ones. She settled down again, her hands massaging her tummy, talking to the baby about sunsets, and cup cakes, and birthday candles, and the pets they'd have.

Talking until she fell asleep.

She was playing with Albert in the little yard, encouraging him to walk towards her, tempting him with his bottle, when Mak appeared. Another green shirt so his eyes seemed greener than ever, his shoulders broad enough to carry any burden, though green shirts couldn't make a man's shoulders appear broad, and the 'carry any burden' part of that thought was nothing more than sentimental nonsense.

She was *not* a sentimental person. The loss of both parents before she'd legally become an adult at eighteen had taught her that bad things happened and sentiment didn't come into it, yet here she was thinking sentimental thoughts.

'He seems to be doing really well,' Mak remarked, leaning over the top rail of the fence, looking for all the world as if this hot, dry, far west country was his natural habitat.

'Physically,' Neena agreed, wishing she'd had a shower and dressed in something better than her ancient red shorts and tattered T-shirt before coming out into the yard.

Then wishing she hadn't thought of that at all! She didn't care, she reminded herself. She was ignoring the attraction!

Which was about as easy as ignoring the sun that was now beating down from the eastern sky, or the dust that whirled around Albert's feet as he gambolled around her.

'Physically?' Mak queried.

Actually, he'd queried it some seconds earlier while her mind had been worrying about her clothing. Now, probably because she hadn't answered, he added, 'Don't tell me you're worried he has mental health problems?'

'Well, he might have!' Neena told him, disliking the smile that lurked behind Mak's words, for all he had a carefully sober expression on his face. 'Not so much mental as emotional. Do you think he knows he's an orphan? That he hasn't got a mother?'

'He probably doesn't know mothers exist and as long as he's fed he probably won't worry about anything.'

But even as he said it Mak knew he was wrong. Camels were herd animals, they were used to company. And she caught him out on it, raising her eyebrows to question his assertion.

'Okay, so he'd be better with company, but the hours you work you can hardly bring another animal in here to keep him happy, especially with Ned away.'

Neena nodded but he sensed her agreement was reluctant, while the look of sadness on her face made him wonder if Albert was the only thing on her mind. She walked towards the gate and he held it open for her so she could lead Albert back into the stable, and being close to her—close enough to drop a quick kiss on her lips—he remembered the kiss of the previous night and wondered what on earth had got into him. The very last thing he needed was to get involved with Neena Singh.

He'd brought up the attraction and while not quite admitting to it, she'd shied away, making it plain she'd prefer it if they both ignored it. In fact, she'd pointed out that there wasn't any other option—a brief affair during his time in town being out of the question.

And she was right, but as he watched her bend over the little camel and saw the taut curves of her backside in the battered red shorts she was wearing, heat stirred in him again.

He couldn't keep showering—it didn't work anyway. He'd get back to work on his thesis—spend his spare time in his room, checking references on the internet, contacting specialists in other countries, maybe get a discussion group going on first response best practice.

He made his way back to the house, walking into the kitchen. Ned was already gone but cereal packets and bowls had been left on the kitchen table. Mak could find his way around the kitchen—did Neena have her one cup of coffee for the day at breakfast? He could put on the machine.

Or maybe cut some fresh roses. The ones on the kitchen table were wilting. Had cutting roses been part of Ned's duties or did Neena like to cut them herself? A quick search of the drawers produced a pair of secateurs and he ducked down the back steps and into the rose garden, where the heavy scent filled his nostrils. There—the dark red ones like his mother grew, the ones the colour of Neena's lips…

Neena left Albert in the stable, glad it was school holidays—she'd get the two Winship kids from down the road to come up and check on Albert for her during the day. They were sensible and big enough to be able to handle him, to take him out into the yard and put him back in the stable, making sure he had milk and water. She'd have to check on when young camels started eating solid food. Perhaps if she left a biscuit of the bale of lucerne hay in his stable he'd nose around and eat it if he felt like it.

As long as it didn't make him sick…

Worrying about Albert's diet occupied her mind while she showered and dressed for the day ahead, but when she wandered into the kitchen, the scent of roses wiped all other thoughts from her mind.

'You or Ned?' she demanded of the man who was fiddling with the coffee machine.

'Me,' he said, and she could have sworn he looked embarrassed. 'Actually, I just went out to get three or four to replace the ones that were wilting, but they were so beautiful I just had to take one of those and one of those and before I knew it I had too many.'

He *was* embarrassed, and there was something so—vulnerable?—about this tall, strong, capable man going mushy over flowers that Neena felt a peculiar twinge in the region of her heart. Not attraction this time—definitely not attraction…

'We'll take some into work,' she said. 'The girls will enjoy having them on the front desk.'

'The girls?' Mak queried, and the smile he offered with the words twisted the twinge thing in her heart.

'They worked for my father,' Neena explained, pouring cereal into a bowl to cover her inner agitation. 'But you'd probably guessed that. When he first came to Wymaralong, no one wanted to work with him—this was a town that wasn't used to foreigners, particularly those of a different skin colour. Helen had been a nurse at the hospital and had retired years before to have a family, but they were all grown up by then so she answered my father's ad and she brought Mildred along. Mildred's husband was the head of the town council at the time, and once Mildred came on board that signalled acceptance to the townspeople.'

'Apart from the fact that they obviously needed a doctor,' Mak suggested, and Neena smiled.

'There *was* that,' she admitted, 'but Mildred and Helen made his acceptance so much easier.'

'And is that why you keep them on?'

Neena studied him for a moment. Was he really interested or was he just making conversation?

'I *am* interested,' he said, correctly interpreting her look.

'I kept them on because they know everyone so well. This was especially important when I first came back to work here and had to get to know people I already knew as people as patients. It was probably even harder for them— the patients—particularly the older men who were suddenly stuck with only one option— well, two if they wanted to drive to Baranock to see a doctor. Mildred and Helen made it easier for them and also taught me so much. They knew which people came in because they needed company and which ones, if they came, must have something seriously wrong because doctors weren't at the top of their popularity lists.'

Mak was frowning at her, looking so distracted she had to ask.

'What?'

He added foaming milk to the coffee cups and passed a cup to her.

'I was trying to imagine the situation. I've always worked in hospitals, so I have no experience in general practice to compare your situation to, but in the ER, ninety per cent of the people we see *are* emergencies. We get the odd person who just wants some attention from another human being, and when we're busy the nurses work a triage system, but it hadn't ever occurred to me that patients in private practice could be graded in the same way.'

It was Neena's turn to frown.

'I didn't mean to trivialise any of my patients,' she said. 'The ones who come in for company or for reassurance are just as important as the others, you know. It just helped me to know their backgrounds so I wasn't wasting time and taxpayers' money ordering reams of tests for people who needed a chat more than they needed medicine.'

Mak still looked puzzled, but as it was almost time to leave for work and she had to phone the Winships and introduce the two boys to Albert, she excused herself and took her coffee through to the office. Talking about medicine, especially the kind of medicine she practised, was such a rarity she found herself enjoying it, and she didn't want to get used to discussing things with Mak—it would leave too big a hole when he disappeared back to the city.

Mak watched her go, being careful to keep his eyes above the level of her backside, although the short skirt she was wearing was nearly as enticing as the shorts had been. He put the dishes in the dishwasher, found some silver aluminium in the pantry and wrapped up half the bunch of roses, but his mind was replaying the conversation they'd had and again he found himself wondering about his career choice—not questioning it exactly, but wondering…

And what had happened to his resolve to put all thoughts of Neena out of his head and concentrate on his job out here, and his thesis when he wasn't working? He left the roses on the hall table near the front door and went into the bathroom to freshen up before they left the house. Today if Neena wasn't busy at the surgery he'd talk to Mildred and Helen about the extra medical workload, and maybe check out the am-

bulance station and talk to the personnel there—
Paul and Pete he'd met, and there were two more.
Someone would be on duty.

One day at a time, Neena told herself as she
came out of her room and saw the roses on the
table. That's all she could do, get through one
day at a time and before she knew it Mak would
be gone and life would return to normal—or as
normal as it could be again once a baby arrived.

'How are you going to manage once the baby
comes? A nanny?'

Neena turned and frowned at the man who'd
come up behind her in the hall while she'd been
smelling the roses.

'Can you actually read thoughts?' she asked him.

His smile awakened the attraction, which
hadn't been all that dormant but had been sup-
pressed enough for her to ignore.

'Worrying about it, were you?' he teased.

'Not worried. I've had plenty of offers, mostly
from mothers of girls due to leave school this
year. One of them, Rachel—the girl, not the
mother—wants a gap year before she goes to
university but doesn't want to go haring off
overseas. She just wants to get some money

tucked away before she hits the big city. She's the eldest of five so has plenty of experience looking after children—even babies—so I've been thinking she might live in. Then there are a couple of others who are regular babysitters around town who will fill in on her days off.' She sighed, then, because it was one of the things she worried about in the night and talking about it might help, she added, 'My main problem is Ned. He's quite convinced he'll manage the baby and the house but he's not getting any younger and it's too much responsibility for him, but he's going to be upset—'

'For Pete's sake, woman, do you worry over every single person in this town?'

Mak's demand was so loud Neena was startled, but before she could protest he was speaking again.

'You worry about people who waste your time because they need a chat and you keep on your elderly staff because you're grateful to them, and you worry about Albert's mental health—'

'Emotional health,' Neena corrected, not liking the way the conversation was going. 'And I'm the local doctor, I *should* worry about people.'

'Not to the extent that it might put your baby at risk. You're right about a newborn baby being too much for Ned—how old is he, anyway?'

'I don't know,' Neena admitted. 'We only knew Maisie was as old as she was because five years ago she got a letter from the Queen and one from the prime minister as well. Our local member of parliament had sussed out her birth date and got hold of a birth certificate. He sent the required letters off to the powers that be and she was delighted. So, given Maisie's age, I suppose Ned must be close to eighty.'

Mak heaved a sigh and headed down the front steps, Neena following. So much for talking about her problems! Far from helping her, she'd only made things more complicated somehow.

Although…

'Why are you so interested in my care arrangements for the baby?' she demanded, reaching the vehicle and turning to face the man she'd thought might help. 'Believe me, they will be beyond criticism in case you're thinking some court might give your sister custody.'

Mak looked at her, dark eyes flashing anger at

him—as soon take a tiger cub from his mother as take her baby from Neena.

'That was the last thing on my mind,' he told her. 'We'd been talking about your work arrangements and I wondered how easy or difficult it might be to get help out here, that's all.'

But he could see she didn't believe him and as they drove in silence the short distance to the surgery, he knew the precarious links of trust he'd managed to build between the pair of them were broken.

Beyond repair?

He didn't know, though even on such short acquaintance he suspected he wouldn't have to wait long to find out. She was a woman who tended to speak her mind.

CHAPTER SEVEN

'FRIDAY I go to Baranock to see my gynaecologist,' Neena informed him, stopping outside the surgery but not opening the door. 'I usually close the surgery for the morning then work afternoons and some evening appointments, but if you want to be on duty you could work the morning.'

Mak stared at her. He'd spent the journey thinking about broken trust and all she'd been worried about had been her patient schedule.

Had he dithered too long that she was speaking again?

'Of course, you might prefer to go out to the site and talk to the different foremen out there or work on your thesis. You're under no obligation to me.'

None of the options she'd offered so far had any appeal, perhaps because he was more worried about the programme she was suggesting.

'You drive the two hours to Baranock and back

then do a full day's work? Aren't you worried about the consequences of getting overtired?'

'And making a bad diagnosis?' she challenged. 'You didn't work twenty-hour days when you were an intern? You didn't get used to going without sleep?'

The dark eyes that he'd seen fired with desire now flared their anger at him.

'I wasn't six months pregnant,' he growled. 'And I wasn't thinking of a wrong diagnosis but of your health.'

'Or the baby's,' she muttered, and now she did open the car door.

He put his hand on her arm to stop her getting out, touching the soft skin, feeling flesh and fine bones beneath it.

'There's another alternative. I'll drive you to Baranock and back. That way you might get to doze on the journey, then we'll share the patients later in the day—or I could do the lot. And I am not thinking *wholly* of the baby, but of your health as well. What good will you be to him or her if you've wrecked your own health before the baby even arrives?'

She studied him for a moment, as if trying to

assess the truth or otherwise of his words, then a smile lit up her face and it seemed to Mak that another sun had risen in the sky.

He forgot the embargo on shaking his head and shook it in disbelief at his thoughts.

'Can we go in your swanky car? It's bitumen all the way—no four-wheel-driving. It's years since I've been in a decent car. I checked it out. Real leather seats! After driving this old loaner and even my tank, it would be bliss!'

Mak shook his head again, now unable to believe that this woman could envisage such delight from something as ordinary as his vehicle.

'We'll go in my car,' he promised, and now she did get out, stepping light-heartedly towards the surgery door, practically skipping with delight. Mak watched her go—he seemed to be doing that a lot these days—just watched as Neena walked away from him, Neena in so many moods, so many guises. How long would it take to get to know a woman like her? A lifetime?

The week proceeded relatively smoothly—well, smoothly compared to Mak's introduction to medical practice in Wymaralong. On Wednesday afternoon, they were called out to another accident on a cattle property where a stockman had been crushed against a fence by a large bullock, but once again it was a matter of stabilising the man before sending him off in a plane to a major hospital.

'With all the callouts like this, wouldn't it be better to always have two doctors in the town?' he asked as they drove back to town.

'Definitely!' Neena's reply was prompt. 'But getting one doctor to stay in a town like this is difficult enough—getting two is virtually impossible. It used to be that the State Health Department employed a doctor full time at the hospital and he had the right to private practice. In those days, he would take in another doctor as a partner so they shared both the hospital workload and the surgery work, and they both made a comfortable living. But with fewer people being treated locally—insurance issues forced the closure of the maternity and surgical wards—the hospital doctor was withdrawn. That happened before my father came.'

'Have you tried to get a partner?'

He was driving, so he could do no more than

glance at Neena as he asked the question. She was looking out the side window, her head turned away, so all he saw was the back of her head and the thick plait of hair. The nerves in his fingers reminded him of how that hair had felt.

'I did once,' she said, still not looking at him. Deliberately? 'Unfortunately he seemed to think that he could share everything—my house, my life, my bed. I suppose if I'd been able to fall in love with him it would have been an ideal situation, but that didn't happen. In fact, he wasn't a very nice man, which is something Ned picked up on from the start.'

'Ned got rid of him?'

She turned now, smiling at him, though it wasn't a real smile, more like something she was trying on for size.

'It wasn't the first time Ned removed an undesirable man from my life,' she said, the smile fading completely as she frowned at her memories. 'After my father died—I was fifteen—I went a little wild. Maisie was in her eighties and she couldn't cope—oh, she kept the house going but she, too, was devastated by my father's death—so Ned stepped in. He got rid of the boy I fancied myself in love with—without recourse to a horsewhip, though that was threatened—and dragged and bullied me back on track. He supervised my homework, came up to school to see my teachers. I suppose what he did was show me that someone cared.'

It had fallen to grizzled old Ned to show the grieving young woman someone cared? Mak didn't consider himself a sentimental man, but the situation Neena had conjured up made him swallow hard.

'You lost your father when you were fifteen?' Mak knew there were other bits of the story that were more unbelievable, but the implications of this one were more relevant to Neena's situation today—or so he guessed. 'Lost both parents so young?'

The smile appeared again, but it held little joy.

'One might be a mistake but two looks like carelessness, doesn't it?' she said, trying to make a joke of something that must still bring her pain. And suddenly Mak understood a little better why she'd chosen to keep the baby, why she talked of it as family—*her* family.

The town came into view and when she looked

up at the tinsel strung across the road between the street lights and said, 'I must get the Christmas decorations up,' he knew the conversation was over, but every little bit of information he gleaned about the woman in the car beside him made him want to know more. It was as if she hid behind a curtain and every now and then lifted a little corner of it so he could take a peek, yet who she really was remained a mystery.

Neena tried to keep her face as blank as possible, although she knew she was frowning inside. For some reason, she kept revealing bits of herself to this man, and she couldn't work out why. It wasn't that he pushed or probed—far from it. He was just there and every now and then she'd feel compelled to come out with something about her past.

He must think she was a nut case the way she kept offering these true confessions—thirty-four-year-old virgin indeed! He'd been right to be surprised. Or had his surprise just been a mask to cover some other opinion he might have of such a sexually repressed woman.

She sighed then regretted it when he said, 'Is the thought of putting up Christmas decorations so tiring?'

Fortunately he was pulling into the car park at the surgery as he spoke—she could get used to this being chauffeured—so there was no need for her to reply. Getting out of the car instead and hurrying inside, hoping they'd be busy enough to not have to see each other for the rest of the day. At least if she wasn't with him she couldn't tell him any more stuff about her past...

But she could hardly avoid him when they got home—the combination of the 'they' and 'home' even in her thoughts causing queasiness in her stomach.

'So, the Christmas decorations—where do you keep them? And don't bother telling me you'll haul them out yourself, because I know Ned wouldn't let you do that and with him away I'm the man of the house.'

They'd checked on Albert and were walking towards the house when Mak asked the question.

More queasiness over the 'man of the house' phrase, but she wasn't going to let him see that.

'They're in a couple of old steamer trunks in the room under the house, but be careful going down there—a snake could have taken up residence.'

'Great! You'd better come with me.'

'To chase the snakes?' she asked, leading him towards the room under the house.

'No, so I can grab you in my arms again to save you. The last time left an impression I'm unlikely to forget.'

Neena turned to look at him, but it was dusk and very gloomy under the house so she couldn't see if he was teasing her or maybe flirting.

'Are you flirting?'

The question just popped out—the same way other things had just popped out since Mak Stavrou had come into her life.

'I might be,' he said, sounding very serious, not flirtatious at all. 'Would you mind?'

'I think I would,' she said, opening the door of the storeroom, turning on the light then standing back and banging an old walking stick on the corrugated-iron walls hoping to frighten any snakes away. 'It's not something I'm good at and last time I tried it I ended up in trouble, so it's best you don't.'

'You don't sound at all certain,' Mak said, taking the walking stick from her and using it to push the boxes and old steamer trunks and wooden chests about on the concrete floor, hoping any snake not frightened by her banging would object to the movement and vamoose.

'About not wanting to flirt?' Neena asked, her voice sounding as puzzled as the expression on her face was.

'Exactly!' he said. 'You think you would mind. That's not a definite no.'

'And *that's* just semantics,' she retorted. 'You know there's nowhere a flirtation can go—you're here and then you'll be gone—what's the point? I might have fallen for one smooth-talking Greek, but to fall for a second one—well, that would be sheer stupidity. Now, are you going to carry those trunks upstairs—the two that say "Christmas Decorations"? Leave them on the front veranda then we'll have a shower and go up to the pub for tea. So far you've only met the sick people in town, it's time you met some healthy ones.'

Going to the pub for tea was not a good idea, Mak discovered some time later. The meal was fine, a good steak with plenty of chips, a bowl of salad served with it, and the people he met all friendly enough, though he sensed this was politeness—it would take along time to become a friend of any of them. A genuine friend, as Neena obviously was, talking to the children who stopped by their table to say hello, asking about their pets, chatting to people at neighbouring tables…

It was after the meal that the fun began.

'You might have told me it was karaoke night,' he complained to Neena as the MC got the music started. 'Do we have to stay?'

'Of course,' she said. 'Not only stay, but as a visitor to town you'll be expected to sing a song. But we needn't stay long. Half an hour at the most. Karaoke not your thing?'

'I can't believe it's anyone's thing,' he growled, 'and there is no way I'm going to sing.'

Unfortunately this statement was drowned out by the MC announcing to everyone present that they were honoured to have the company of the new doctor in town and asking if he'd do the town the honour of singing the first song.

To have refused would have looked churlish so, fighting the flush of either embarrassment or anger that was wanting to surge into his cheeks, Mak stood up, walked to the small stage and took the microphone.

'Do you have a favourite?' the MC, a youth who didn't look old enough to be in a pub, asked him, scrolling the available song titles on the screen.

'How about "Tie me kangaroo down, sport",' Mak asked and saw the look of surprise on the lad's face.

'You know that?'

'Let's say I know a student version of it so I know the tune, and if the words are up on the screen I can sing them rather than the rude ones.'

'Well, okay,' the young fellow said, although he still seemed uncertain that a doctor should be singing such a song.

Presumably the pub patrons felt the same way, for they listened in total silence as Mak launched into the song. He glanced towards Neena and saw she was trying not to laugh, but then the audience joined in the chorus and they were away, everyone shouting out the words of the song. He finished to a roar of approval and loud clapping and, embarrassed by the attention, hurried back to the table, accepting pats on the back and 'good on yous' on the way.

'Well, a man of many talents,' Neena greeted him. 'You've won a lot of hearts with that song—

well, you won them over just getting up to sing, a lot of strangers would have refused.'

'The other doctor?' Mak queried, though he wasn't sure why the memory of the man who'd wanted to share Neena's bed lingered like a bruise in his head.

'Oh, he would never have lowered himself to eat at the pub, let alone join in the karaoke.' She answered easily, most of her attention, Mak guessed, on the new singer up on the stage, a young woman with a sweet voice, singing a popular country and western ballad. But as the song finished and Neena stood up to leave, she looked at him and said, 'Why on earth would you be thinking of him?'

Mak wondered the same thing himself, but rather than admit it, he just shrugged, said goodnight to the people close to them and followed her out of the pub. Outside, the main street was deserted except for an occasional car driving slowly past. They'd walked the couple of blocks from the house to the pub, so set out to walk back, Neena leading him down a side street then along a lane at the back of the houses.

'A lot of outback towns have these lanes,' she

told him, as the warm darkness enveloped them. 'In the old days, everyone kept goats for milk and meat and the goats grazed on the town common by day. Every evening the goat boys would go out and herd them back to town and they'd come down the lanes and into their own back yards. Today, of course, there are feral goats—descendants of the originals—through-out the west.'

Mak tried to imagine it, the goats coming in a herd down the lane, two or three dropping off into the back yards of the houses. The big pepper trees under which they walked would have been saplings then, and the streetlights in the main street gas—if indeed there had been streetlights.

'You like it here?' he asked, although he really knew the answer, hearing it her voice when she spoke of the town and its people.

'It's home to me,' she said.

'But you went to the city to study. Weren't you tempted to stay there?'

She stopped and turned towards him, and though they were in shadow and he couldn't see her face, he could guess at the expression of dis-belief she'd be wearing.

'Down there with all the noise and pollution and traffic and people?' she queried. 'They were the worst years of my life. I was lost. I hated it. All I wanted was to come home, but I had to stay because the people here had faith in me—they believed in me and had made it possible for me to go away and study.'

'But you admitted you felt under an obligation to them. Surely that coloured your decision to return?'

She shook her head.

'No, it might have had I found I loved the city, but as it turned out, I knew it wasn't right for me. All I ever wanted to do the whole time I was there was to come home.'

He heard the loneliness she'd felt in those years in her voice and couldn't help himself, putting his arms around her and drawing her close.

'Poor little homesick Neena,' he said softly, but the physical contact was reawakening the desire he'd been at pains to keep at bay, and as his body heated he held her more tightly, then dropped a kiss on the top of her head.

She didn't slap his face or move away, so he let his lips roam lower, kissing her forehead, her temple, brushing his lips across her eyelids, learning the feel of her face, the shape of it, through the movement of his mouth across her skin. Right up to her lips…

Move, Neena told herself, but her legs wouldn't obey the instruction and the rest of her body remained locked in Mak's embrace. There was something mesmeric about the feel of his lips on her skin, the taste of him as his tongue probed into her mouth. She let him kiss her and from there it was only a very small step to kissing him back, feeling her body come to life as she explored his lips with hers, her hands also exploring now, pressing against his solid back, sliding down to more slender hips, the curve of his buttocks filling her hands.

'I could make love to you right here and now,' he whispered, adding more fuel to the fire already burning within her.

'Not a good idea,' she murmured, lips to lips, not moving even a fraction of a centimetre.

One of his hands had slid between them and was fondling her breast, sending tremors of delight directly to the nerve centre of her sexuality. Now she was moaning against his mouth and though her head kept yelling at her to stop, to move away, she could no more move than she could deny the attraction she felt towards this man.

Her body yielded to the moment, thoughts banished as she revelled in the delights physical attraction could provide. Heat swelled her tissues, and blood throbbed through her veins, her body pulsating with a need she barely understood and had never felt assuaged. Her lips began their own exploration, moving across his cheek, along a jaw slightly rough with emerging whiskers. The feel of that roughness intensified her excitement, and she slid her hands beneath his shirt and felt the contrast of the smooth skin on his lower back, the hardness of his backbone…

'You are beautiful, and you are driving me to distraction!' Mak growled the words as he eased away from her. 'I know all the reasons this is impossible as well as you do, yet it's equally impossible for me to keep my hands off you.'

Neena felt the coldness of separation—the shock of it—a sense of loss.

He had slung his arm around her shoulders and, holding her close, was meandering on down the lane, chatting away as if this was a perfectly normal conversation.

'And it *is* impossible—what could it be but a brief affair? Then there are the complications of the baby, but what I can't decide is whether kissing you from time to time—I'll try to restrict myself to darkness and odd moments—is going to make things better or worse.'

They walked on in silence for a few minutes, then he spoke again.

'Don't you have anything to add to this conversation?'

The lane had ended at a cross street and her house was just ahead. Mak's arm dropped from around her shoulders, although Neena was reasonably sure there was no one around to see them.

More loss!

'I don't think so,' she said, unable to keep a touch of tartness out of her voice, 'but, then, thirty-four-year-old ex-virgins don't have a lot of experience to draw on in situations like this.'

He halted under a streetlight and looked down at her, lifting his hand to run a finger down her cheek.

'Did it bother you a lot, the virginity thing?'

He was frowning at her, as if really interested

in her answer, but with the tension of his presence still firing all her senses, all she could do was shrug it off.

'I never thought about it,' she said. 'Well, not often. Everyone has bad days when they're tired and out of sorts and when I was like that I sometimes wished I had someone I could whinge to.'

His frown disappeared and he laughed out loud.

'That's the best reason for getting married that I've ever heard—to have someone to whinge to!'

'Well, it's true—that's how I felt!' Neena told him crossly. 'And I don't see anything funny about it.'

'We should be back in the lane so I could hug you,' he said. 'I'm not laughing at you but at the simplicity of it. Most people think of marriage as a sharing of joys but you're absolutely right, having someone to complain to when things are going wrong *is* important.'

But for some reason, him agreeing with her didn't make Neena feel any better. In fact, it made her feel worse so she strode away, taking the front steps two at a time, reaching the top before she realised she hadn't checked on Albert. She turned to come back down but Mak halted her with a hand in the air.

'I'll check on him,' he said, and Neena wondered if having someone to check on Albert for her might be nearly as good a reason for marriage as having someone to whinge at.

Not that it could be—at least, not with Mak...

And now she knew Mak, would she be happy with an alternative?

It was such a weird thought that she opened up the steamer trunk to distract herself and began to delve through the Christmas decorations. What colours had she used last year? Red and green, she rather thought. So this year maybe gold and white, garlands with gold bells and white flowers hanging off them along the veranda, and tomorrow she'd sort out the lights and put up the Christmas tree then decorate it with white and gold baubles.

Mak came up the steps, reported Albert was asleep and opened the other trunk.

'Wow, you really do Christmas in a big way. Look at all the decorations.'

He pulled out a bag of scarlet flowers, and

another bag of red balls, going through the contents of the trunk with the excitement of a child.

'No, I'm going white and gold so anything that's not white or gold, just put back,' Neena told him as he opened up a huge red paper bell.

'No red?' he queried, waving the bell at her, and once again Neena felt a twinge of loss. Hanging Christmas decorations with someone would be nice as well.

'You can pull out any green garlands,' she told him. 'We can thread them around the veranda and put the white and gold decorations in them.'

They worked amiably together for an hour, decorating the front veranda so people walking by could see they'd made a start.

'We'll leave the rest for tomorrow,' Neena said, when the strain of this unnatural togetherness had become too much for her. 'Do you want a cup of something or a cold drink before you go to bed?'

'I'll fix something for myself in a minute,' Mak said, getting back up on the small stepladder to adjust the tilt on an angel he'd put above the door. He'd climbed down as Neena slid past him—or almost slid past him.

'Hoy!' he said, touching her arm to halt her

escape. 'That's mistletoe up there with the angel—you know what that means.'

And before she could object he was kissing her again. Worse still, she was kissing him back! Again! Somehow he shuffled them into the hall so they weren't clearly visible to anyone walking by, but their lips remained joined and their bodies fitted into the contours of each other's as if they already knew the bumps and hollows.

Mak held her close and his mouth consumed hers, stealing her heat and tasting her passion, desire enveloping them both. Neena began to tremble under the spell of it, her body firing, melting, aching, a need for fulfilment she didn't fully understand sending tremors deep into her belly.

He wanted to share my bed!

The stark phrase she'd used so recently echoed in Neena's head and she broke away, muttering it out loud, so Mak looked at her with an expression of shock and distaste. A black frown drew his eyebrows together, growing anger evident in his face and the tension of his body.

Well, she couldn't help that! She escaped to her bedroom and collapsed on her bed, so confused by her emotions she didn't know where to start thinking about them.

'Was I the one who said we couldn't have an affair?' Neena asked, watching the fan lazily stir the air above her. She ran her hands over the bump. 'How foolish was that, huh, Baby Singh?'

But deep in her heart she knew having an affair with this man to whom she was so attracted would only make the parting, when it inevitably came, far harder. Better to put up with a little frustration now than an agony of regret later.

The problem was that it was more than a little and, she suspected, more than frustration. Frustration she could handle, but this aching loneliness that seemed to have permeated every cell in her body, that was something else.

But she was used to loneliness—personal loneliness—so why now was it upsetting her?

Resting her hands on Baby Singh's bump, she considered it—well, not for long, because she really knew. Without any conscious effort on her part—and, to be honest, not much on his—she was falling in love with Mak. For a while she'd put it down to attraction—to some late-developing part of her suddenly becoming aware of her sexuality—but in her heart she knew it was more than that. Talking to the man, working with him, discussing patients and medicine in general, an insidious idea had slid into her mind—not to mention her body—an idea that this was good, better than good, special.

That this *might* be love!

Her sigh reverberated around the room, hanging on the blades of the fan and washing back over her...

Mak was experienced enough to know if he'd kept kissing Neena in the hall the inevitable conclusion would be that they'd have ended up in her bed. And now she'd put a stop to it, he somehow felt ashamed of himself—as if, some time in the future, she might remember him, too, as a man who'd wanted only one thing—to share her bed...

Which he did, of course, but he didn't want her remembering him that way—speaking of him with the same distaste she'd used when speaking of that other man...

He strode along the hallway to his room where he sank down on the bed and rubbed his hands across his face, trying to banish the taste of her from his lips, and all thoughts of her from his mind.

Maybe she *was* a witch!

The thought didn't help—bewitchment wasn't going to go away any more than desire was.

Desire?

Or lust?

Wasn't that all it was?

He pictured her in his mind and knew it wasn't lust—what he felt for her was more complicated than lust.

Much more complicated!

CHAPTER EIGHT

NEENA rose early, mixed up enough formula to see Albert through the day, then took it out to the stables where she filled his bottle and put the rest in the small refrigerator she'd turned on out there. She walked the little camel around the yard, chatting quietly to him, but her head was wondering where things stood between herself and Mak Stavrou while her heart was wondering if it really was love or if it was just an overheated reaction to romantic kisses in a darkened lane.

Whatever it was, head and heart agreed that seeing him again would be awkward, working with him maybe worse than that, but her morning chores accomplished, she had to return to the house, to shower, dress for work, have breakfast then get about her business. Life went on no matter what was happening in the hidden depths of one's heart.

Was it symptomatic of just how confused she was that she dithered in front of her wardrobe, and instead of pulling on a skirt and cotton knit top—her usual work-wear—she considered a white cotton dress she'd bought on impulse in Baranock one day. It had a lacy insert across the bust and hung in soft folds below the insert, so it was cool, but for all its shapelessness, kind of sexy.

A work dress it was not! No, but she *could* wear it to Baranock on Friday when they went, and maybe while she was there check out the little boutique where she'd bought it and see what else they had. Maybe a Christmassy kind of dress—or something sleek and slinky.

Sleek and slinky when she was six months pregnant?

Ashamed of her own thoughts, she grabbed a denim skirt and pale blue, sleeveless T-shirt and pulled them on, this fantasising about her wardrobe so bizarre she didn't want to think about what might be causing it.

'Good morning.'

Didn't have to think about what might be causing it—he was sitting in the kitchen!

Mak sounded relaxed and friendly but, then, stopping the kiss probably hadn't caused him the slightest anguish so how else should he sound?

She echoed his greeting, surreptitiously eyeing him in an effort to gauge his mood.

As well try to read the mood of the table, Mak's face gave away as little, his hazel eyes meeting hers momentarily then moving on as he crossed to the bench to start the coffee machine.

Neena helped herself to cereal, added milk and a tub of yoghurt, some slices of mango…

'Did you slice the fruit?' she asked, surveying the platter that held not only mango but rock-melon, orange and peach slices.

And now he smiled, a real smile for it lit his eyes and caused such ructions in Neena's heart and lungs and stomach she wished she hadn't spoken.

'I told you I could cook,' he said.

'So you did,' she managed, then concentrated on her breakfast, refusing to look at him again.

'So what excitement is on the agenda for today?' he asked, and she had to look at him.

'More of the same. I'd like to be able to tell you that Thursdays offer some variety but as you have probably gathered by now, most of our variety comes from emergencies and the fewer I have of those the happier I am.'

He nodded.

'Well, in that case I might take the day off from the surgery and visit the ambulance station, then go out to the powerhouse site again. I can find out how many people they are expecting to employ out there both short term and long term. Is that all right with you?'

It was Neena's turn to nod, which she did, because although she'd been uneasy about getting through the day in Mak's company, the thought of not having him around made her feel even worse. Not that she hadn't asked for it—firstly breaking away from the kiss last night then, to make matters worse, putting Mak in the same category as the horrible doctor she'd employed years ago.

'It's probably a good idea,' she agreed, although she knew the pause between his conversation and her response had been far too long.

No more was said, so Neena finished her breakfast, put her plate and cup in the dishwasher and left the room, going through to her bathroom to clean her teeth and put on lipstick before heading to work.

'Well, I'm off,' she called from the end of the hall. His answering, and supremely casual, 'Bye' slammed into her chest like an arrow.

So it was gone, the rapport they'd built between them. And just like Dr Horrible—to say nothing of Theo—it had all been about getting her into bed. Depression threatened to descend like a thick black cloud, but as she crossed the veranda and saw the decorations there—a lot of them decorations her father had bought for her as a child—she pushed it away. She was a strong, independent woman, for all she'd been tempted to think in terms of togetherness by kisses so subtle, yet so hot, just thinking about them warmed her body.

Or maybe that was just the midsummer sun, already burning on her skin and parching the ground across which she walked. If she hurried she'd have time to go up to the hospital before she started work. If Mr Temple was still stable she'd send him home, but make sure he had his tablets in packs with the days and times to take them clearly marked.

She arrived at the same time as a nurse from the retirement village pushed a wheelchair in through the emergency doors—Maisie.

'I phoned your house and got Dr Stavrou. He said you'd already left and I guessed you'd come here. Maisie's had a really bad night.'

Neena was already bending over her old friend, talking quietly to her as she checked her pulse and listened to the rattling agony of every breath.

'Will you at least let me put you on oxygen?' she asked, and Maisie nodded, so Neena followed the two nurses as they wheeled Maisie into a ward and settled her into bed.

'It's time for me to go, Neena,' Maisie whispered, and Neena bit back the tears she longed to shed, opting instead for briskness.

'Nonsense! You can't go before Christmas, you'd spoil the holiday for too many people. And then there's the baby—you have to wait to see the baby.'

Maisie smiled, but her eyes closed and although her breathing was easier once Neena inserted a nasal cannula, she didn't open them again, drifting off to sleep, or possibly into a light coma.

'I'll phone Ned, he's out at the Harrises',' Neena said, patting Maisie's hand then moving away because duty called, no matter that she longed to sit with the beloved old woman for the final hours of her life.

Ned said he'd be in as soon as he could and Neena was saying goodbye to Lauren when the phone rang again.

'Dr Stavrou for you,' Lauren said, handing Neena the receiver.

'Hello!'

The word was probably as wary as Neena felt. He was supposed to be on his way out to the site, or at the ambulance station, not phoning her.

'Lauren told me about Maisie,' he said, his deep voice coming so clearly over the phone it sent shivers down Neena's spine. 'I'm sure you want to stay with her, so I'll go to the surgery. I've plenty of time to do the other visits. You sit tight and I'll handle the patients.'

What could she say?

'Thank you.'

It didn't seem enough but just saying those two words made a lump form in her throat and she had to swallow determinedly before speaking at all.

'Don't mention it,' he said, all business, so matter-of-fact she had to wonder if his previous plans for the day had been no more than an excuse to avoid her company.

She returned to sit beside Maisie, taking her hand and talking to her about the adventures and joys they'd shared.

'Remember that boy in primary school who was always pulling my plaits,' Neena murmured. 'And you went up to him as he walked home and told him you'd pull something else of his, and hard, if he didn't leave me alone. I never knew what you were going to pull, not until we got into high school and had our sex education talks. Can you imagine a young girl today not knowing what boys looked like until they were thirteen?

'And the time in sixth grade when I had to take something I'd cooked myself and you said chocolate crackles were the only things I'd be able to manage but it was midsummer and by the time I got them to school they were a mess of chocolate, Copha and rice crisps in the bottom of the cake tin.'

Neena kept talking, holding Maisie's hand, aware she probably couldn't hear the conversation but wanting her dear friend to know she was close by anyway, so the things they'd laughed over together all got another airing, the remember this, remember that of so many shared years.

'You know she wouldn't want you crying.'

Ned had arrived and his chiding voice made Neena aware that tears were sliding down her cheeks, and probably had been for some time.

'Maisie always let me cry—she said crying got the hurt out,' Neena reminded him, although Maisie might not have used the same philosophy on her son.

But Ned just nodded and sat down on the other side of the bed, bending forward to kiss his mother's cheek, gruffly letting her know he was there. And now they both remembered, sharing reminiscences of the woman who had brought both of them up, until Maisie's breathing changed, and finally stopped altogether.

'She was a good woman, the best,' Ned said, then he looked across at Neena. 'You okay?'

She took a deep breath and nodded.

'I will be,' she told him, and knew it was a promise. Her life had gone off track but it was time to get it back in order—Maisie had loved order and had taught her charge to believe in it as a basis for a good life. Neena owed it to Maisie to take control once again.

Though perhaps not right now, a smaller,

needy Neena deep inside her whimpered. Do I really have to?

'I'll do the certification and whatever has to be done.'

Mak's voice made her turn, frowning, towards the door.

'What are you doing here?' she demanded, order gone before she'd even begun to get it back.

'I asked Lauren to phone me when it happened so I could do what has to be done. It's lunchtime, I'm not holding up any patients.'

Neena just stared at him, her heart so full of gratitude she couldn't speak, but Ned could.

'Thanks, Mak,' he said. 'Come on, little girl, I'll take you home.'

This time Neena managed a smile.

'It's a long time since you called me that, Ned,' she said, new tears oozing from her eyes and trickling down her cheeks. 'Lately it's been "stupid woman"!'

'Which you were,' he reminded her but he put his arm around her and led her away from Maisie's bed. 'But even Mum agreed that everyone's allowed a bit of stupidity in their life. Come along.'

Neena went home with Ned, where they sat down and discussed Maisie's wishes—no funeral, no service, just a private cremation, 'and if either of you turn up I'll come back to haunt you'—then her ashes to be scattered on the hill where the statues were.

'We'll say goodbye to her there,' Ned said, 'and if friends want to come, that's okay, but as she always said, she'd outlived all her real friends by so much that the only people she knew now were people who really didn't know her at all.'

'You and I did,' Neena protested, but she had always known what Maisie had meant—that the people she'd really loved had gone before her...

So they talked until the shadows spread into the room, when Ned reminded her he had animals to care for and should be going.

'You go, I'm all right,' Neena told him, but Ned still hesitated, showing an uneasiness so rare in Ned Neena guessed it had nothing to do with his mother's death.

'That fellow Mak—he's not bothering you?'

The question made her want to laugh at the absurdity of it. 'Bothering her'? As if the muddle

226 GREEK DOCTOR: ONE MAGICAL CHRISTMAS

in her mind and the chaos in her body could fit into a mild word like 'bother'!

Oh, he might be tantalising her, tormenting her, frustrating her and generally disrupting her life, but bothering her?

'No, he's not bothering me,' she told Ned.

The man who wasn't bothering her returned to the house as she was putting the finishing touches to the Christmas tree. She'd set it up, as Maisie always had, in the bow window in the living room so the lights of it could be seen from the street.

Why she was putting it up at all, she didn't know, but it had given her something to do, and in doing it she remembered her old friend and carer, for it was a task they'd shared for so many years.

'I picked up a pizza at the café,' Mak announced as he walked in, the smell of cheese wafting from the box he carried. 'They assured me there that you liked anchovies.'

His hazel eyes were studying her—gauging her mood? Her grief?

'Thank you,' Neena said. 'For the food, for

thinking of it, for today at the hospital, for today at work.'

'Nonsense, it's what I'm here for, but you really do need two doctors in this town, even without the workers out at the site. What do you do for time off? How do you manage then? Are there locums available? Do the flying doctors provide that kind of cover? What happens?'

He was sounding crosser and crosser as he fired the questions at her, but Neena could only shake her head.

'Can we eat while I answer?'

He looked taken aback for a moment, then he grinned at her.

'Sorry, but although there wasn't one emergency today, it finally sank in how difficult it must be to run the practice on your own. And once the baby arrives it will be impossible.'

Uh-oh! He'd remembered why he was really here—to take over the baby's life. Neena was following him into the kitchen, drawn by the smell of the pizza and the fact that it seemed a long time since she'd eaten, so the realisation did no more than warn her to be wary. She *had* to eat, and an argument now would spoil the food.

'I've got a locum booked while I take maternity leave and I'm hoping he or she might like the place enough to want to stay.'

'You don't know who you're getting as a locum—don't know if it's a he or she?'

Mak was slapping plates on the table, his voice rising in disbelief as he asked the question.

'I've booked one through an agency,' Neena explained, watching the slices of pizza land on her plate and wondering if she could pick one up and start on it before Mak sat down.

He found the roll of paper towels and plonked it in the middle of the table and finally did sit, but before she could start eating he was questioning her again.

'And is that satisfactory for the town? Having a stranger of whom you know nothing coming in to take your place?'

She looked at the pizza and sighed. No chance of eating until she'd sorted out what was really bothering Mak. It couldn't possibly be the locum.

'The town is used to locums. After my father died they went for ages without a doctor at all, then the government stepped in and we had a series of locums, some good and some not so good, and in the years since I've been practising, I *have* been away at times, mostly to attend conferences to help update my skills and knowledge. And yes, I know the town needs another doctor and I have, from time to time, tried to find one, but it's not that easy.'

She glared at him across the table.

'Satisfied?' she demanded. 'Now can I eat?'

'Go right ahead,' he said, but she knew she hadn't touched on whatever lay behind his bad mood. Well, too bad, she hadn't had that great a day herself. She took a bite of pizza and found it had been seasoned by something wet and salty. Surely she wasn't crying again.

'Bloody hell!' Mak was on his feet, angrier than ever, striding around the table, lifting her from the chair then sitting down on it with her on his knee. 'I'm sorry, I shouldn't be upsetting you today of all days, and you need to eat. Lauren said you'd had nothing all day. Here, let me wipe the tears.'

He ripped a paper towel off the roll and dabbed at her cheeks then lifted a slice of pizza and held it to her lips. 'Eat!' he commanded, and she took a bite, chewed and swallowed then took another,

her body stiff with tension, afraid to relax against Mak's bulky warmth in case all the attraction stuff started up again.

Not that it hadn't already, for he'd rested one hand against her hip and heat was radiating out from it, sprinting along her nerves and puddling in her belly.

'I'm sorry I was cross. That's the last thing you needed today. It's just that spending only one day doing your job on my own, I got to realise just how hard it must be for you—how impossible, really. I mean, I read all the time about the problems of getting doctors in country areas and, worse, keeping them there, but the realities of the job these country doctors do just doesn't come through in those news stories. I mean, who else is there to certify the death of a loved one for them? It's ridiculous you have no back-up, no support.'

Neena shifted on his knee, sure her weight must be bothering him, wanting to move but enjoying the comfort of his solid body.

Enjoying the heat!

'It's not that bad,' she protested, her mouth still half-full of pizza.

She should move, get off his knee. She'd stopped crying, so why keep sitting there?

Because it felt so good?

No, that was a reason to move!

'We manage—me and all the other doctors running single-practitioner practices out here in the bush.'

'I'm not worried about all the other single practitioners out here in the bush, I'm worried about you.'

He was stroking her back now and the rhythmic touch was so soothing—so hypnotic—Neena wanted to lean back against him and forget everything but the feel of his body and the warmth of his arms around her.

But this was Mak Stavrou. She'd let one of his family get close to her and—

'Worried about me or the baby?'

The words popped out and though she regretted them immediately they couldn't be recalled.

He was cursing, or at least she assumed that's what it was, for the flow of words were presumably in Greek and he'd stopped stroking her back, which made her feel sad.

She should move.

But as when she'd decided that the first time, nothing happened.

'Forget the baby!' He'd finally reverted to English. 'Let's just keep this conversation about us.'

'Oh, Mak,' Neena sighed. 'You must know there can be no us.'

'Because of some presumptuous idiot you once employed, or because of my nephew, who seems to be known around town as The Rat?'

Mak's voice was pure steel, and though now the conversation had turned nasty and her legs might have obeyed an order to move, he'd wound his arms around her, tucking her hard against his body, making escape impossible. His hands rested on the bump and she knew he must feel the baby kicking.

'Because our lives are so far apart.' It was a weak response but she'd had to say *something*.

'So we don't even explore the attraction between us? And don't bother denying the attraction, Neena. We'd have ended up in bed last night if you hadn't inconveniently remembered the other doctor.'

Now she moved, turning on his lap so she could

see his face, see his eyes burning with intensity as they fixed on her face.

'Is that all you want? To explore the attraction? To end up in bed?'

He cursed again and drew her close once more.

'Why does everything I say to you end up sounding like that?' he muttered, the words muffled because his lips were pressed against her head. 'No, it isn't all I want. I want to know you, and not just biblically. I want to learn more about you—like the anchovies on pizzas and why you've never cut your hair and what it is about this place and its people that has such a strong hold on your heart. Little things and big things and, yes, sex is part of it, part of getting to know you, but it's not just about sex.'

He paused then added, 'And it's definitely not about the baby. It's about you and me. Maybe we'll discover that there's nothing more than the attraction, but if we don't, if the attraction leads to deeper emotions, then we'll work out the geographical problems and any other problems—together.'

Neena could feel the tears starting again and blinked them back. She answered the least consequential bit of Mak's statement, because that was about all she could cope with right now.

'My father liked my hair long—my mother had long hair, I suppose that's why.'

Mak laughed and she could feel the deep chuckle as a movement in his chest. Feel his ribs, and the muscles that encased them, feel the strength of his legs—feel his desire…

Desire!

'And it *is* about the baby,' she added sadly. 'Though not in the way that you mean. It was my fault, the pregnancy—but in the beginning, it was all about exploring an attraction—'

His fingers found her lips and pressed against them.

'It takes two to make a baby and I don't want to know.'

She sighed, but now she did move. As if she could tell Mak about that night with Theo—tell Mak what his nephew had done…

She stood up on the pretext of getting a glass of water and took the chair across the table from where he now sat.

'I wouldn't have taken you for a coward,' Mak said, as she selected another piece of pizza.

She put it down on a piece of paper towel, the delicious aromas that had tempted her now making her feel nauseous.

'A coward?'

The green eyes were on her face, studying her intently—seeking a lie or evasion, she was sure.

'Isn't that what you are? Aren't you hiding from life behind one bad emotional experience? Aren't you living vicariously through other people's lives because you're afraid to have a life of your own? Oh, I can understand it—you'd lost your mother when you were so young, then to lose your father as a teenager, for a long time you'd have been too wary to get close to anyone, lest you lose them, too. Is that what happened with Theo—did you send him away? Or did you fall in love with him and when he walked away—as Theo surely would—you suffered another loss and decided that was it?'

He was waiting for an answer, the mesmerising eyes demanding one.

'I thought you didn't want to know,' she snapped, angry because a lot of what he'd said was probably true. 'What do you want me to say? Yes, your psychobabble about my avoiding relationships is spot on? It probably is, I've considered it myself, and as for Theo—as for your precious nephew—well, I did explore the attraction and then, at the end, I decided the exploration had gone far enough. I knew he was as shallow as he was clever and charming, I knew his sole aim was to get me into bed, and though I thought I'd be able to go along with it, for the experience if nothing else, at the last minute I decided not to—I said no.'

She took a breath, thinking it might calm the anger, but it was too white hot to stop.

'Theo took it as a tease, we struggled a little, and that's probably when he lost the condom—and I lost the struggle. What's done is done. The baby's mine, not yours or your family's. Goodnight!'

She stormed out of the room before she made a total idiot of herself by bursting into tears.

Again!

Mak sat in the kitchen and swore some more, not that it helped.

Theo had raped her!

The implications of it loomed so large in his head he couldn't think about it, although for the first time he didn't feel sadness over his nephew's death—he felt regret the wretch wasn't alive so Mak could kill him himself.

How had she handled it?

Who would she have turned to? Not Ned or Maisie—she was too protective of them.

No one! He knew that was the answer. She hadn't reported it to the police, or Theo would have been charged and the family would have known.

So she'd kept it all inside her where most of her hurts seemed to be.

His heart ached as he thought of her situation—alone in a way he could never imagine. Then discovering she was pregnant!

How could he not shake his head? So much fell into place now, especially Neena's reluctance to have anything to do with his family.

Feeling totally useless and inadequate, Mak tipped the remnants of the pizza—more than half-uneaten—into the bin and tidied the kitchen. More than anything he wanted to go to Neena, to hold and comfort her.

Comfort she wouldn't accept—not, at least, from him.

He left the house, checked on Albert, then took

to the streets, hoping to walk off the tension
and—yes, anger in his body. He was in the
darkened lane, his anger beating out the rhythm
of his strides when his mobile trilled in his
pocket. Habit had kept it on him, although he
hadn't expected to receive any phone calls.

'Have you talked to her about giving me a
proxy for the shares?' Helen's voice demanded,
and Mak, who'd been reliving the kiss he'd
shared with Neena in the lane, was jolted out of
his reverie.

'No!'

Well, what else could he say?

'But it's what you're there for,' Helen bleated,
and Mak forbore from reminding her that her
original story had been a keen interest in her
unborn grandchild. 'The cousins have called an
extraordinary general meeting for the third of
January—the woman should have got a notice of
it from the solicitors. She'll have a copy of the
notice and a proxy form and an agenda for the
meeting, including notice of motions. The
cousins want to merge with a big power
company but first they have to vote on a new
board chairman—well, with Dad dead we have

to do that anyway—but if one of them wins the vote, they'll take Hellenic in a different direction. This talk of a merger is just an excuse to sell it off! We owe it to Dad, Mak—*you* owe it to Dad!'

And although aware she was dumping a classic guilt trip on him, Mak couldn't help but accept a little of it. His father *would* have loved Mak to follow him into the business, his father *would* have hated seeing the business go out of family hands…

'I'll talk to her,' he promised Helen, though he wasn't sure just how he could follow through on the promise. As if the bloody shares mattered, given the enormity of what Neena had suffered.

And was possibly still suffering if she hadn't had counselling, or sought help of some kind…

CHAPTER NINE

NEENA set the mood for the day as Mak entered the kitchen to find her already there, sipping at her weak coffee.

'Coffee maker's on, and I found some fruit bread in the freezer. I'm having it toasted for breakfast as a change from cereal. I left it on the bench so if you want some, help yourself.'

He studied her for a moment—a slim, small figure huddled in a bathrobe in a kitchen chair, her plait hanging over one shoulder. Her attention remained fixed on her toast, and the magazine she was leafing through. So this was how it was to be. No mention of the revelations of the previous evening, no further discussion of Theo, no further discussion at all!

And in spite of having a thousand questions, Mak decided to play along with it. After all, what *could* he say? I'm sorry my nephew raped you? Hardly!

'What time do we need to leave?' he asked, as he brought his coffee and toast to the table and sat down opposite her.

Now she looked up, dark eyes half-hooded, dark shadows beneath the eyes causing a physical pain in Mak's chest.

'And don't tell me you'll drive yourself,' he added, before she could protest. 'You're exhausted, and driving in that state would not only put you and the baby at risk but could endanger other lives. At least with me driving you might be able to sleep.'

She nodded and returned her attention to the magazine.

'Time?' he prompted.

'Eight-thirty.'

She stood up, put her coffee cup and toast plate into the dishwasher and left the kitchen, the voluminous bathrobe Mak hadn't seen before wrapped tightly around her slight body.

Sadness enveloped him. He'd felt something for this woman that had sneaked past his defences and filled empty spaces in his soul and now, before he'd had time to explore where those feelings might go, he'd lost her.

Although maybe not, he decided a little later. It was eight twenty-five and he was beside his car, opening the door to let in some fresh air before they took off. Neena came tripping down the steps, right on time, and smiled at him. Not a full-blown, isn't-life-wonderful, Neena kind of smile but it wasn't a polite mask of a smile either.

Hope sneaked into his heart, then he remembered the revelations of the previous evening, and despair slammed into hope and left it reeling.

Hope had been foolish anyway, he told himself, holding the car door for his passenger and trying not to see the way the lacy stuff at the top of her dress revealed her full breasts.

They drove out of town in silence, Mak wondering how and when he could raise the issue of the rape, something he suspected she needed to talk about.

'This is bliss—not only being driven but being driven in such luxury!'

The softness of her voice—the genuine delight in it—was the last thing Mak expected. He glanced towards the woman he'd been expecting to stay silent for the two-hour drive and saw a genuine smile.

A wholehearted Neena smile that made his stupid heart skip a beat!

And *that* made him angry.

Well, not angry, but uncomfortable.

'Is that it? You tell me last night that my nephew raped you and this morning all you're concerned about is being driven in a good car. And for your information, it's not *that* good a car!'

She turned to him, and he saw the shock on her face.

'Did you not expect me to talk about it?' he continued, his gruffness evidence of his emotion. 'Is that how you handle all your problems? By ignoring them? If what happened to you had happened to a patient, what would you have done? What would you have suggested?'

Now she frowned.

'You mean reporting it to the police, getting counselling, that kind of thing?'

'Of course I mean that kind of thing. What did you do? How did you get through it? Who did you turn to? Who helped you?'

He knew he was sounding angrier and angrier

but he couldn't help it—the thought of her emotional pain and trauma was like a red-hot poker in his gut.

'Well?' he demanded, when the silence had gone on too long.

'I thought it all through myself,' she said, her chin tilted to match the defensiveness in her words and the defiance of her pretty dress. 'I considered all the options, though not the reporting business. That was never one of them, although it did make me understand why other women might opt not to report such things. I had agreed to do it, Mak. I had told Theo yes. I know that sounds stupid and pathetic but I'd decided I didn't want to die a virgin—that I wanted to experience sex at least once in my life. I knew Theo for what he was—I knew there was no future in it—and that was probably why I decided he'd do for the—'

She stopped and Mak took his eyes off the road for long enough to glance her way. Her skin was pale and her hands were twisting tightly in her lap, and although he wasn't a psychologist he suspected this confession, though hard, might be good for her—cathartic.

'Experiment,' she finally said, adding, 'Because that's all it was, an experiment.'

'You still said no,' Mak growled.

She nodded, and turned to look out the window, but not before he saw the tears streaming down her face. He pulled over, got out of the car and walked around to her side, lifting her out and sitting back down with her on his knee, holding her, murmuring to her, mostly in Greek because they were the only words he could use in this situation—words of love she wouldn't understand.

Gradually he felt her tense body relax against him, and she took his hand and held it against the bump.

'You haven't asked,' she whispered, while he marvelled at the feel of the baby kicking against his palm.

'About why you kept it?'

'Yes!'

He held her more tightly.

'That part I think I understand. You had Maisie and Ned for family, both of them getting old, and though the whole town treasures you, you had no one of your own.'

'Selfish, wasn't it?' she muttered with a defiant little sniff that nearly broke his heart.

'No way!' He held her more tightly, then kissed her on the neck. 'You are the least selfish person I have ever met, and you have so much to offer to a child, not least of which is wholehearted, abundant love.'

Her body, which had tensed, relaxed against him once more and Mak felt if they could sit like this for ever he would be happy, but the practical soul he knew lived inside Neena moved them on.

'We have to go—I'll be late for my appointment.'

He kissed her cheek, then stood up and turned to deposit her back in her seat, walking around the car and getting back behind the wheel.

Was she feeling better?

He hoped so, because he wasn't. He was more confused than ever. The only certainty seemed to be that the last person Neena would ever see as a possible lover was the uncle of the man who'd raped her—charming, immature, bloody Theo!

'No wonder he left you the shares—talk about conscience money!'

Rage at his nephew's behaviour had forced the

words from his lips, but as soon as they were out he regretted them, for Neena was frowning at him.

'I'm sorry,' he muttered, 'but I get so angry just thinking of it. He was a grown man—he knew the meaning of the word no. And how dared he think that willing the baby some shares would make things up to you in some way! He wasn't expecting to die, which makes it one more empty gesture.'

'We should talk about the shares,' Neena said quietly. 'After all, it's why you're here.'

'Not any more, it isn't,' Mak growled. *'Nothing!* Nothing our family could give you would even begin to make restitution. The shares are the baby's and what you do with them as trustee until he comes of age is entirely up to you.'

'But I need to understand things in order to know what to do,' Neena persisted. Mak flicked a glance at her and saw a little frown on her face. 'I need to talk about it, Mak, and now seems a good time.'

'Did you open the solicitor's letters?'

She shook her head, which was what *he* wanted to do.

He sighed instead.

'Short version—my cousins, who are also shareholders, want to merge the business with a bigger concern. Having the experimental power station coming on line in the not-so-distant future has vastly increased the value of the company and vultures are circling.'

A huge wedge-tailed eagle lifted off the ground as he spoke, some unidentified piece of roadkill dangling from its talons.

'Apt timing,' Neena said, nodding at the bird, then peering upward through the side window to watch its flight. 'But are these companies vultures? Might they not be good for the business?'

A sense of shame washed over Mak as he realised just how far he'd detached himself from the family concern. Early on, he'd always read the annual reports and he'd made sure he kept abreast of new developments—mainly so he could discuss things intelligently with his father—but in recent years medicine had begun to dominate his life more and more, and Hellenic Enterprises had slipped into the background of his life.

And now he had to admit it.

'I truthfully cannot say.'

'Yet you'd like me to give you the baby's proxy?'

He shook his head, dismayed by the impassable rift that had developed between them.

'I have never said that, but if you did you can believe I would look at all the information available about the proposed merger. I would not fail your child by using the proxy irresponsibly.'

'But you'd be drawn to vote with your sister?'

Mak sighed.

'My father built the company from nothing. My sister has worked under him since she was at school, learning from the bottom up. Yes, my sister would like the family to retain ownership and, yes, there is sentiment involved because my mother has taken my father's death very hard, and for her to see us lose the company he lived for would make things worse.'

He paused, glanced towards his passenger, but she was staring straight ahead and her profile told him nothing of her thoughts.

Well, here goes!

'But for all of that, should you offer me the proxies, I hope I would still make a judgement based on sound business principles rather than emotion.'

Now she turned to face him, the little frown he hated seeing furrowing her brow.

'I'm not at all sure that's the answer I wanted to hear,' she said, shaking her head as if perplexed by it. 'My focus for this baby has been about family—it's because of family that I didn't kick you out that first night, because, no matter what, you are the baby's family and as I don't have an extended family then it seems to me your family can give him that. But will you destroy your own family—and it *would* cut you off from them—by voting for sound business principles if that's how it turned out?'

Mak threw his hands up in the air, though only momentarily, re-grasping the steering-wheel almost immediately.

'What do you want of me? What do you want me to say? Is there any way I can win in this ridiculous situation? Read through the information yourself, I'm sure there'll be something in there about the merger. Vote the baby's proxies yourself—leave me out of it!'

I wish I could, Neena whispered, but only in her head. She had been so determined to be happy, to put the previous night behind her, to enjoy this time out in Mak's company, to revel in being driven in his lovely car, and now it had all been spoilt.

It was her own fault—revealing all that anguish stuff last night. Had the sadness of Maisie's death brought it all bubbling to the surface again? Had that one extra loss proved too much for her?

No way! She was stronger than that! And it was probably just tiredness that had tears leaking from her eyes. Again!

She turned towards the window so Mak wouldn't see them and, not wanting to rummage in her handbag for a tissue, lifted her hand to wipe them off her cheeks. Did she sniff that Mak grabbed her hand, felt its dampness, swore, braked and pulled the car onto the shoulder of the road?

Without a word he got out, stalked around the bonnet, opened her door, unsnapped her seat belt and all but hauled her out for the second time.

'Women!' he muttered, shaking his head and producing a perfectly laundered white handkerchief with which he proceeded to mop her tears. 'Honestly, you get a man so tied up in knots he doesn't know which way to turn.'

He peered down at her as if searching for an

elusive droplet of water, then, apparently satis-fied, he shoved the handkerchief back into his pocket and leaned forward to kiss her lips. A gentle kiss—a don't-cry kiss—that's all it was, although it made the tears start again.

'Stop that right now,' he ordered, taking her into his arms and holding her hard against his chest. 'I know you need to cry, to grieve for Maisie—and to grieve for a lot of things—but I'm equally sure you don't want to arrive for your obstetric appointment with swollen red eyes. What's more, I can't concentrate on driving with you weeping silently beside me. Tonight we'll go up to the hill near the lake and you can cry all you want there, okay?'

He looked so fiercely earnest Neena had to agree, breathing deeply and banishing the tears.

'Good,' he said, and kissed her again, then, as her lips responded, the kiss deepened until the hot, dry, desert landscape disappeared from around them and it seemed to Neena they were afloat on a cloud of joy and softness, fluffy and white, a cloud made just for two. The past with all its sadness was for-gotten, and physical sensations so sublimely new and interesting they made her shiver stole through

Neena's body. She pressed closer to Mak, her mind lost in the sensations he was generating, sadness burned away in a kiss.

'Sunstroke,' she muttered as she broke away from him, and collapsed on weakened bones back into the car seat.

'Sunstroke?' he echoed, reaching in to wrap the seat belt around her.

'Only thing that could explain the weird flights of fancy in my head,' she mumbled, and though Mak looked puzzled he seemed to accept the explanation.

He took his seat, belted up and started the car back along the road to Baranock.

'We'll sort it all out,' he said, somehow making the words sound like a promise, and although Neena wasn't at all certain what 'all' they could sort out, she decided to believe him and relaxed again, seeking and finding the pleasure just being in the car—with Mak—had given her earlier.

'Still adamant you don't want to know the sex?' her obstetrician asked, when she'd completed her examination and run through all the questions she asked every visit, ticking off the positives and not finding anything negative in Neena's pregnancy.

'Still adamant,' Neena told her. 'I want the surprise.'

'She doesn't even hint at what it is?' Mak asked when Neena passed the conversation on to him a little later. They were sitting in a small café in the main street of Baranock, Mak drinking coffee while Neena sipped a strawberry milkshake.

'No, she's very good, although I know she'd love to tell me, but I can't help feeling if I know the sex then I might start getting preconceived ideas about him or her.'

'Yet you talk about it as a him,' Mak probed.

Neena grinned at him, unable to believe they were so relaxed together after the tension that had formed earlier in the car.

Not to mention last night…

'I think him sounds better than it, don't you?'

His answering smile tugged at her heart, but she knew it was like the sunstroke image of the two of them alone on their cloud. Nothing could come of this attraction for so many reasons, but that didn't mean she couldn't just relax and enjoy his company today. One day soon, perhaps even tomorrow, she'd read through all the unopened letters from the solicitors and think about whatever they contained, but for now she was just going to enjoy Mak's company and the drive back to Wymaralong—a little capsule of time alone with him.

Neena had been dozing so the oath woke her, and she looked up to see the trailer on the cattle train ahead of them swaying dangerously.

'He's going far too fast,' she whispered to Mak, her eyes mesmerised by the sway of the trailer, fortunately empty of cattle. 'We need to get past him.'

'We'd never make it. He's taking up all the road. We'll drop right back.'

He braked sharply as he spoke, but it was too little, too late, for the momentum of the swaying trailer had tipped the rig, and with metal screeching and dirt flying everywhere the rig rolled, the trailer coming adrift, skidding back along the road, slamming into the car within a beat of Mak's evasive swerve.

Blackness everywhere, blackness and noise. Noise she couldn't understand—people yelling, men's voices—idiot—too fast, she's pregnant…

Who was pregnant?

She was pregnant. She tried to feel the bump, to find Baby Singh, but the blackness was solid and she couldn't find her hands.

'Neena, can you hear me? I've got your hand—your left hand. I'm squeezing your fingers. Squeeze my hand if you can hear me. Neena, talk to me.'

Someone saying her name—asking her to squeeze her hand. Where was her hand? Left hand, he'd said. How could she tell right from left in the dark like this?

How could she find her hand when she couldn't even find her baby?

She wanted to cry but she'd promised Mak she wouldn't cry until later. Who was Mak? Why couldn't she cry till later?

She squeezed both her hands—or she thought she did. She must have done something for the voice was telling her how clever she was, urging her to talk.

'Where's my baby?'

'Neena, the baby is all right, I'm sure of it. We can't get at you, but I've felt all around and he's still there where he should be. I've felt a kick, so he's okay, now concentrate on you. Are you hurting anywhere?'

Was she?

She didn't seem to be but in the dark it was hard to tell.

'Dark!' she managed, then she was floating on a cloud, all fluffy and white, floating on a cloud with Mak and he was kissing her and it was the most beautiful, delicious, delectable sensation she'd ever experienced.

'We *have* to get her out! She could be haemorrhaging to death under there for all we know. She's pregnant, we need to get to her.'

Mak was squatting low on the road, his arm shoved through an incredibly small space in the crumbled sedan, clinging to Neena's hand. He was yelling his frustration at the fire crew wielding the rescue equipment, although he knew yelling wasn't helping anyone. He'd never seen men move more slowly, cutting here, snipping there, carefully peeling back bits of wrecked trailer and his car as if every piece was a sacred relic. It had taken them for ever to remove the drums of molasses that had been in the trailer when it had swung in an irrational but deadly arc straight into the passenger side of his vehicle.

And all he'd been able to do had been to watch in horror as the woman he'd grown to love had been encapsulated in death and destruction. That she was still alive seemed a miracle—if she *was* still alive!

He squeezed her fingers but her hand lay still and motionless in his. Dark! She'd said it was so dark…

'Okay, that's the last piece of the trailer, now we'll cut through here, attach a wire rope to there…' the fire-crew boss indicated the windshield frame of the car '…and pull the trailer and the top of the car off in one piece, which means we need you out of the way in case the whole shebang comes crashing back down.'

Mak gave the cold fingers one final squeeze and moved reluctantly away, but only far enough to be safe if the load collapsed. He held his breath as the tow-truck winched the wreckage upward then, as it inched forward, tearing the metal with teeth-clenching screeches, finally leaving a clear passage to the front seat of the car, Mak darted forward, ripping away the torn side and front airbags, the lover beating the doctor by seconds as he touched Neena's face with trembling fingers before feeling for a pulse beneath her chin.

She was alive!

Think first response—think pregnancy implications. The foetus is extra-sensitive to changes in blood oxygen levels. Mak clamped an oxygen mask across Neena's face while behind him the ambos and the fire crew all protested.

'You can't start oxygen while we're cutting and shifting metal because of the sparks,' someone said.

'Then stop cutting and shifting for a few minutes while I stabilise her. She's pregnant, the baby needs oxygen—they both do.'

He felt her pulse again, mainly because it had been such a strong beat earlier he thought he might have been mistaken but no, the beat was still strong—and steady!

'Neena, can you hear me?'

An ambulance attendant was wiping the thick dark molasses from her face. She was drenched in it, the beautiful white dress a mess.

Yet her pulse was strong!

Mak grabbed a stethoscope from one of the

ambos and pressed its diaphragm against her belly. He heard the foetal heartbeat and felt another kick. The ambo was sliding a backboard in behind Neena's body while another tried to fit a cervical collar.

'I can't get at it,' he said. 'Her head's trapped. Does she have long hair? Is that what's caught somewhere?'

Does she have long hair?

Mak saw the shining curtain of it in his mind's eye, felt the silk of it against his fingers, but knew they had to move her.

'I'll cut it,' he said, his heart racing because he knew what pain the loss of her hair would cause her. But emotional pain was better than death and they had to get her free as quickly as possible. For all her steady pulse she could be bleeding internally—bleeding externally, for that matter. There was still only a small part of Neena and the baby visible.

He talked quietly to her as he cut, using heavy shears someone had handed him, telling her it would grow again, that everyone would still love her just as much—that he'd still love her.

'Stand clear, Doc, we do this part best,' the ambo said when he'd cut the hair.

He stood clear, though he longed to gather her in his arms and lift her out, to hold her close for ever. But these men were the experts at moving injured people, so he bit back his impatience and watched.

'Unbelievable,' one of the ambos said, as they strapped Neena onto the stretcher. 'When I saw the way the trailer had landed on that car I didn't think anyone would have survived, yet there's hardly a mark on her, apart from all the molasses that must have spilled from the drums in the trailer.'

And no indication of internal injuries, although she was slipping in and out of consciousness, which Mak didn't like.

'I'll ride with her,' he told the ambos as they loaded her into their vehicle.

The older of the two men smiled.

'Thought you might want to do that,' he said. 'Looks to me as if Wymaralong might have two doctors again.'

Mak opened his mouth to protest. Of course he couldn't stay in Wymaralong. He was a specialist ER doctor, his life was in the city. But one look at the grey-faced woman on the gurney made him wonder, and as he sat in the back of the ambulance, using wet tissue to clean the muck from her face, the idea of becoming a country doctor instead began to grow on him.

Although wasn't he assuming too much?

What made him think Neena would want him?

A couple of hot kisses?

She'd never said she loved him but, then, he'd never told her how he felt—hadn't known it for sure until he'd seen that trailer careening towards them and had known, no matter what he did, it was going to hit Neena's side of the car.

Then he'd known. He'd felt pain judder through his body and had yelled his futile protest. Oh, yes, then he'd known…

CHAPTER TEN

'I CAN'T stay here in hospital. There's nothing wrong with me. I've got patients to see.'

She was still in the ER at Baranock hospital and already protesting that she wanted to be released. Mak looked at the slight figure beneath the sheet on the ER examination table, at the angry cuts and abrasions the accident had left on parts of her body and the mess thick in her hacked-off hair.

'Your obstetrician is on her way and she's already said she wants to keep you in for a few days' observation. You've had a shock, the baby's had a bad jolt—'

Neena sat up, her hands automatically cradling the tight bump of Baby Singh, panic in her voice.

'Placental abruption! I need an ultrasound. What if my placenta's come adrift and the baby is suffering?'

'The staff here have done an ultrasound and

everything's fine,' Mak soothed her. 'But the obstetrician will repeat it just to be sure. Relax, and be thankful you've both come out of it so well, but be sensible as well, and stay here to rest.'

'But my patients!' she wailed, and Mak shook his head.

'I would never have taken you for a wailer,' he chided. 'I'll look after your patients and, believe me, that's a sacrifice. I'd far rather be here looking after you.'

'Looking after me?' Neena frowned up at him, suspicion gathering in her foggy brain. 'Why should you want to be here looking after me?'

Mak smiled at her—a funny kind of smile that made her stomach feel distinctly queasy.

'Don't you know?' he said quietly. 'Don't you really know?'

She shook her head, which was when she realised something else was wrong. Her head felt light—unanchored. More weirdness. She forgot about Mak's puzzling question and lifted her hands, feeling her hair, all knotted and thick.

'I need a shower. My hair's a mess.'

Her hands continued their exploration as she spoke, continued to feel for her plait…

'It's gone—my hair's gone!'

Panic raced through her body, panic and despair, and yes, again a loss—too much loss. There'd just been too much loss…

Mak was speaking, something about having to cut it off.

'You cut off my hair?' she yelled at him, sitting up so she could see his face more clearly. 'But I told you why I kept it long—I remember telling you. It was *my* hair and, yes, it was a nuisance but I loved it.' She fell back down and closed her eyes, adding in a whisper of grief, 'And you cut it off!'

'It was only hair,' the nurse who stood beside Mak murmured quietly, but Mak wouldn't accept her empathy. He shook his head.

'It was more than that to Neena,' he said. 'It was her link to the past, to her family, to a family she lost when she was far too young.' He began to walk away, then turned back to the nurse. 'After the obstetrician's been, would you help Neena shower and maybe get someone in to neaten the ends of her hair so it doesn't look quite so bad when she sees it?'

The young woman gave him a peculiar look but she nodded her agreement.

Mak was leaving the hospital—he was ninety per cent sure Neena was okay but he'd phone the obstetrician later—when he ran into Lauren.

'I was doing my last-minute Christmas shopping here in Baranock and heard about the accident,' she said. 'Is Neena okay? The baby?'

Mak nodded, then knew Lauren needed more information.

'By some miracle, both are fine,' he said. 'Her specialist is due to check her out any minute but we—well, I—had to cut off her plait to free her from the mess and she's devastated about it.'

'It's hair!' Lauren said, and Mak smiled.

'I know that and you know that, but Neena?'

Lauren nodded.

'She grew it for her father. It's funny because we all rely on Neena to be the sensible one—the rock. When things go wrong in Wymaralong, whether it's a lost dog or a major disaster like a house fire, we turn to her for guidance and support and she's there for everyone, but she's never had anyone to lean on, apart from Maisie and Ned—and she's lost Maisie. Now her hair— it's a bit like Samson in the Bible, isn't it? Maybe she's lost her strength with it.'

Mak found he wasn't as concerned about the hair as he was about the image of Neena Lauren had conjured up—the image of the woman who had no one to lean on. Yet she'd decided to go ahead with a pregnancy that, in the beginning at least, must have caused huge emotional turmoil in her, and she'd held her head high in the small town, though talk would have been rife.

Would she lean if there was someone there to lean on?

Lean on him if he was there?

Lauren was still talking, something about popping in to see Neena then giving him a lift back to Wymaralong.

'You will come back, won't you?' she added anxiously, and Mak smiled.

He'd never find out if Neena would lean unless he was there, now, would he?

'Of course,' he told Lauren. 'I'll find a rest room and clean up a bit then would love a lift back to town. I'll phone the girls at the surgery and tell them to put the afternoon patients back a bit. What time, do you think?'

Lauren did the sums in her head and announced they'd be back by four-thirty, then she dashed away to check on Neena.

Mak moved more slowly, uncertain where this decision was taking him but knowing it was the right one.

Neena lay on her back in the hospital bed in Baranock, the sheet pulled up to her chin, so the bed was neat, apart from the bump of Baby Singh. She had her hands clasped around the bump and one part of her mind was whispering fervent thanks that he was okay.

All the time!

As for herself, she was clean, her hair, what there was of it, washed and gleaming, her head still feeling incredibly light. She had pads on her eyes because spilled molasses had got into them and though it had all been flushed out, her eyes still stung.

Apart from that, she was fine. She'd even slept for a while—or maybe more than a while because it was dark outside now.

So everything was okay.

Except that it wasn't.

She wasn't!

She was edgy and unhappy, and though part of that was because she was doing nothing—you will lie there and do nothing for at least two days, her obstetrician had ordered—and doing nothing didn't come easily to her, but the major part of it was that Mak wasn't there.

Which was stupid considering she barely knew the man!

He'd been in her life for what—six days? And she was missing him?

Get real!

Get over it!

Be pleased he was good enough to go back to Wymaralong and fill in for her. Most professionals, after the introduction he'd had to bush doctoring, would have seen her safely into hospital and headed back to the city.

Except, of course, there were the shares.

Had they come to some decision about the shares? She remembered talking about them on the drive to Baranock but couldn't remember what, if anything, had been decided.

Though she did remember a kiss—a wonderful kiss—so wonderful she'd felt as if she was floating on a fluffy white cloud—or maybe that had been part of the accident. How could they have been kissing on the road to Baranock with Mak driving?

But something must have happened because when she thought about the drive—or the shares, come to that—she felt hot all over and a softness radiated out from between her thighs and she had to move uncomfortably on the bed for all the specialist had told her to lie still.

The phone interrupted her thoughts, and she heaved herself up until she was sitting against the pillows before answering it. It would be Ned, for sure—checking on her—ready to nag about her not looking after herself, although it hadn't been her fault.

'Hello! Are you there, Neena?'

Not Ned at all—Mak!

Neena smiled at the phone.

'Neena, can you hear me?'

He was sounding anxious, which made her smile some more, but the third time he demanded to know if she was there, she realised she'd better answer him.

'Yes, I'm here,' she said.

'Well, try a hello next time you pick up the

phone,' he grumbled. 'I thought you'd passed out or fallen out of bed or something.'

He sounded so cranky she had to laugh, which didn't help his crankiness one bit.

'I was phoning to let you know that everything went well at the surgery, I've seen all the patients—nothing urgent's happening, and the obstetrician said you're okay but you have to rest. You *will* rest, won't you? You won't go wandering around the hospital offering advice and comfort to all the other patients.'

'I *will* rest, Mak,' she promised him, wishing again that he was there so she could see by looking at him if he was as anxious about her as he sounded or if he was just being a fussy doctor.

'Good, I'll come to see you on Sunday—if anyone crashes a helicopter the ambos can look after him—and Lauren said there's an ambulance going to Baranock on Monday to take someone down for surgery, so you can come back with them.'

He was coming to see her on Sunday?

Coming to see her but not to take her home?

Coming to see her to talk about her patients and Saturday surgery, or coming to see *her*?

'Neena, are you there?'

Again the demanding tone.

'Yes, I'm here,' she said, although the smile inside her was so all-encompassing she couldn't think of anything else to say. Fortunately he didn't seem to expect a conversation for he ordered her to keep resting, promised to phone again the next day and said goodbye.

Altogether a very strange conversation, but she was still smiling so it must have been okay.

By Sunday Neena was reconciled to her hair, in fact, she rather liked the way the new short style framed her face and swished around her head when she moved it. And although she'd obeyed the 'rest' orders of both the specialist and Mak, she had persuaded one of the nurses to visit the boutique and get her a couple of pretty night-gowns and a loose floaty dress in fine cream cotton that she could wear back to Wymaralong on Monday.

She was wearing one of the pretty nightgowns now, although she didn't really expect Mak to drive all that way to visit her. Well, she half expected he would, because he'd phoned three times on Saturday and each time he'd said he would.

She actually didn't know what to think about Mak…

Mak felt stupid. He was dressed in his cream chinos and his best green polo shirt, the one Helen had given him for his birthday because, she said, it would make his eyes look greener.

Neena had probably never noticed he had green eyes.

And she'd think the bunch of roses he had gripped in his hands were a silly idea when she was coming home the next day.

And he didn't even know if she liked chocolates, for all the check-out girl in the supermarket had assured him she did.

Though why the girl had assumed they were for Neena was another thing he didn't know.

So he stalked through Baranock hospital, roses and chocolates in hand, mind in total confusion, so although the directions had been simple he lost the way three times. Then there she was— sitting up in a bed at the end of a four-bed ward—

looking so incredibly beautiful for a moment he was sorry he'd come.

Why?

Because he'd driven for two hours practising all the things he wanted to say to her, and now he was here he was tongue-tied.

He couldn't possibly be tongue-tied. He was a well-educated professional—he had words for all occasions.

He was tongue-tied.

She smiled at him, which didn't help one bit.

'Are those for me?' she asked, her smile growing wider, though whether because she liked the roses or was delighted to see him in such a dither, he couldn't tell.

'From the garden,' he managed, although she'd have known that from the moment she saw them. 'And these—I hope you like chocolates.'

She smiled again and thanked him, but the smile and the look of her, the clear olive skin of her chest and shoulders rising out of the gathered neckline of her nightdress, the sharp bones of her face, the shapely red lips—the beauty that stole his breath every time he looked at her—was too much.

He sat down on the bed and took both her

hands in one of his, then touched his other palm to her cheek.

'I love you, you know,' he said, and watched her eyes widen in wonder. 'I didn't know until I nearly lost you—well, perhaps I knew, but it was all so awkward, and it happened so suddenly I had to be suspicious of it, but it's love all right, because nothing else could make me feel so totally stupid, so ill at ease, so at a loss as to what to do or say or how to act or anything.'

The words dried up and he stared at her, desperate to find some reaction in her face, her eyes.

Nothing!

He'd made a complete fool of himself and she felt nothing!

The silence lasted a year and a half then he had to break it.

'Have you got nothing to say?' he demanded, as the discomfort of the silence and his own idiocy stirred a kind of anger in his chest.

She smiled again, then whispered, 'No.'

'No? That's it? No you don't love me?'

She reached out and touched a finger to his lips.

'No, I've got nothing to say,' she explained.

'What can I say when you've stolen my breath— the same way you stole my heart?'

And she leaned forward and kissed him, gently at first then with increasing passion, so the very least he could do was kiss her back.

Did 'stole my heart' mean she loved him? the part of his mind not concentrating on the kiss wondered.

The kiss seemed to be telling him she did, so he intensified the exploration of his lips and tongue and held her closer, one hand resting on the bulge of the baby, guarding it as he fitted her body to his in the way he knew was meant to be.

Applause from the other beds eventually made him break away and, though hugely embarrassed, he stood up and took a bow for both of them.

'We've just got engaged,' he explained to the three watching and applauding women.

'Well, given the size of her, I'm glad about that,' one of them said, but most of Mak's attention was on the woman in the bed by the window. He hadn't actually asked her to marry him, had he?

'Did I ask you in the nervous ramble when I came in?' he asked, sitting down on the bed but far enough away from Neena that kissing couldn't start again.

'I don't think so, though love was mentioned,' she told him, taking his hand and holding it tightly. 'And, anyway, Mak, can we really be engaged? Can we really take these feelings further? I can't leave Wymaralong, not only because it's the place of my heart but because of what I owe the people there. Not that they ever expected repayment for their generosity, but it's what I want to give them. And you belong in a city hospital—your skills and training, every-thing you've worked for, mean that's where you should be.'

It was a problem Mak had been struggling with himself for the past two days, and although he hadn't fully worked out a solution, he knew there were options available that could make his pro-fessional life in Wymaralong as fulfilling as he needed it to be.

'I'm sorting that out,' he told her, shifting so he could tuck her close to his body, their backs to the audience in the ward. 'I've been working on my master's because I want to teach, and a lot of teaching these days can be done over internet links. Lectures can be put on the 'net and as long as the students have some face-to-face sessions during the year, that's all they need. I can keep up with the first response research, and if the week I've spent at Wymaralong is anything to go on, I'll still be getting plenty of hands-on experience. On top of that, the town needs two doctors—why shouldn't one of them be me?'

Neena was tempted. It all sounded so wonderful it was hard to believe.

'The baby?' she asked, because he had to get a mention.

'The baby will be mine,' Mak said firmly. 'I will be the only father he or she will ever know. Later we can talk about Theo and explain as much or as little as you want to explain, that's up to you, but the baby will be mine.'

'Really?' Neena asked, unable to believe things could be this simple.

'Really,' Mak said, and he kissed her again, long and hard, so she had no breath left to argue with him over it.

But after he'd gone, with the coming of darkness, doubts grew and although Neena told herself there was no way Mak would be committing himself to her and to Wymaralong for the sake of shares in the family company, the spectre of doubt hovered over her head.

So much so she rummaged through the information stored under 'not needed right now' in her brain and came up with the name of the solicitor who had been in touch with her over Theo's will, and as soon as offices opened in Brisbane next morning, she was on the phone to him.

'No, you cannot give the shares away or sell them. They are to be held in trust for the baby, so really, until he or she reaches his or her majority, you must hold on to them.'

'And vote them in the case of business decisions?' Neena asked.

'You will hold the proxies and you can vote them yourself or give your proxies to someone else should you so wish.'

Mak would be the obvious choice, Neena thought as she hung up the phone, though Mak knows little of the business.

Time to start taking control of her life again. She phoned the surgery and asked to speak to Mak.

'And put the phone down in Reception,' she told Mildred. 'I'll hear if you keep listening.'

Mildred huffed then put her through and Neena heard the click of the disconnection.

'Do you really want to marry me?' she demanded of the man on the other end of the phone.

'I do,' Mak said, so circumspectly Neena knew he had a patient in with him. Well, too bad.

'And do you really love me?'

'I do,' Mak said again, as if already practising for a wedding. 'Didn't I tell you that when I phoned this morning?'

'Yes, several times,' Neena told him. 'I just wanted to be sure.'

'Be very sure,' Mak said, and the conviction in his voice sent shivers down her spine.

She said goodbye and phoned Information, then dialled a number and asked for Mrs Cassimatis.

'And who shall I say is calling?' a snooty receptionist demanded.

'Tell her Dr Singh—Neena Singh from Wymaralong.'

'Helen Cassimatis!'

The voice was brisk and businesslike, but Neena sensed the hesitation in it—hesitation that sounded very like fear.

This was confirmed with Helen's next words.

'Has something happened to Mak?' she asked, her voice faltering with anxiety.

'Oh, dear, I didn't mean to frighten you. Mak's fine,' Neena assured her, then hesitated, uncertain how to proceed. Fortunately Helen spoke again.

'Mak tells me I may have misjudged you. I'm sorry.' The words were quiet but they held real regret and had a ring of sincerity that made Neena swallow hard.

'I may have done the same to you,' she admitted huskily. Then she took a deep breath and began again. 'That's why I'm phoning.'

'Oh, yes?'

Neena smiled to herself. This sounded more like the Helen of the emails—brisk and confident. Another deep breath and Neena plunged ahead.

'I'm phoning to ask you and your mother to come out for Christmas. You can fly to Baranock and I'll have someone meet you there. Mak tells me you usually have a family Christmas and you've been too busy with work to organise it so I wondered if the two of you might like to join us out at Wymaralong.' She hesitated then added, 'Spend Christmas with your family-to-be.'

The silence at the other end stretched to infinity then back before Helen said, 'Do you mean that—about the family-to-be?'

'I do,' Neena told her. 'The baby will need a grandmother and you're the only one available, and a great-grandmother, well, that would be so special. So what do you think? Wymaralong for Christmas?'

More silence then a muffled voice.

'I can't talk now because I'm crying but I'll phone tonight. I've got Mak's mobile number, I'll call him.'

'No, don't do that,' Neena said quickly. 'I want your visit to be a surprise. I'll phone you.'

'Thank you,' Helen said, her voice still thick with tears. 'Thank you so much.'

Pleased with her morning's work, Neena rode up front in the ambulance on the return trip to Wymaralong, and though she wanted to go to the surgery she'd promised Mak she'd go straight home and keep on resting.

'Best for Baby Singh,' he'd said.

'Best for Baby Stavrou,' she'd corrected, and had heard his sigh of pleasure.

* * *

For Christmas, Neena slipped the proxy papers in a cylinder and wrapped them like a bon-bon, put Helen's name on them and put them under the tree. For Mrs Stavrou she had some pretty jewellery her mother had brought from India. It had been around long enough to become fashionable again but as Neena never wore jewellery herself, she was happy to give it to the older woman.

Mak raised his eyebrows at the growing number of parcels under the tree but showed no interest in reading names or cards, so her surprise was safe. Mak actually showed little interest in anything other than work and being with her, touching her, holding her, kissing her, and now that he was convinced she was well, even sleeping with her, although the first few nights they shared a bed precious little sleeping went on.

'I do love you, you know that,' he said for about the millionth time. It was Christmas Eve and she was preparing a picnic supper to take up to the hill above the dam.

'I do,' she said, stopping the preparations of a simple salad long enough to give him a kiss. 'Now, go down and check on Albert while I finish here. You know Ned's joining us up on the hill, and the girls from the surgery, and Lauren and her family.'

She didn't tell him Ned had driven into Baranock earlier to collect his mother and his sister—for that was her Christmas present to him, his mother and his sister joining them for the celebrations—a family time for all of them. And though the nerves in her stomach were so tight she worried about Baby Stavrou's comfort, she knew it would be all right because the love that had grown between herself and Mak was strong enough to leap any hurdle.

An hour later they all stood, Helen, Mrs Stavrou, Ned, Mak and her friends, and watched the sun go down over the red desert landscape. They raised their glasses and toasted the sunset, then toasted the future—Mak and Neena's future, Hellenic Enterprises' future, and the future of the little town in the far outback of Australia that now had two doctors.

EPILOGUE

THE baby gave a cry and Mak let go of Neena's hand to turn and take the still wet bundle from the obstetrician.

'A baby girl, for all your conviction,' he teased his wife as he handed her the baby and watched her hug the precious bundle to her breast.

'Well, we've already got a boy with Albert, so a baby girl is good,' she whispered, touching the wrinkled face with a gentle forefinger. 'Don't you think?'

She looked up at Mak with so much love in her eyes he felt his heart move in his chest. This was stupid. They'd been married nearly three months now and he still felt strange tugging movements in his chest when his wife looked at him! Shouldn't he be over that?

He sat down beside Neena and probed a finger at the newborn child, who turned dark blue eyes in his direction. Then one scrawny arm moved and her tiny hand grasped his probing finger and held tight, and his heart bumped around in his chest once again.

'My two girls,' he whispered, not ashamed of the tears that filled his eyes and clogged his voice. 'My two beautiful girls.'

MEDICAL™

Large Print

Titles for the next six months...

June

SNOWBOUND: MIRACLE MARRIAGE	Sarah Morgan
CHRISTMAS EVE: DOORSTEP DELIVERY	Sarah Morgan
HOT-SHOT DOC, CHRISTMAS BRIDE	Joanna Neil
CHRISTMAS AT RIVERCUT MANOR	Gill Sanderson
FALLING FOR THE PLAYBOY MILLIONAIRE	Kate Hardy
THE SURGEON'S NEW-YEAR WEDDING WISH	Laura Iding

July

POSH DOC, SOCIETY WEDDING	Joanna Neil
THE DOCTOR'S REBEL KNIGHT	Melanie Milburne
A MOTHER FOR THE ITALIAN'S TWINS	Margaret McDonagh
THEIR BABY SURPRISE	Jennifer Taylor
NEW BOSS, NEW-YEAR BRIDE	Lucy Clark
GREEK DOCTOR CLAIMS HIS BRIDE	Margaret Barker

August

EMERGENCY: PARENTS NEEDED	Jessica Matthews
A BABY TO CARE FOR	Lucy Clark
PLAYBOY SURGEON, TOP-NOTCH DAD	Janice Lynn
ONE SUMMER IN SANTA FE	Molly Evans
ONE TINY MIRACLE...	Carol Marinelli
MIDWIFE IN A MILLION	Fiona McArthur

™ MILLS & BOON®

MEDICAL™

Large Print

September

THE DOCTOR'S LOST-AND-FOUND BRIDE	Kate Hardy
MIRACLE: MARRIAGE REUNITED	Anne Fraser
A MOTHER FOR MATILDA	Amy Andrews
THE BOSS AND NURSE ALBRIGHT	Lynne Marshall
NEW SURGEON AT ASHVALE A&E	Joanna Neil
DESERT KING, DOCTOR DADDY	Meredith Webber

October

THE NURSE'S BROODING BOSS	Laura Iding
EMERGENCY DOCTOR AND CINDERELLA	Melanie Milburne
CITY SURGEON, SMALL TOWN MIRACLE	Marion Lennox
BACHELOR DAD, GIRL NEXT DOOR	Sharon Archer
A BABY FOR THE FLYING DOCTOR	Lucy Clark
NURSE, NANNY…BRIDE!	Alison Roberts

November

THE SURGEON'S MIRACLE	Caroline Anderson
DR DI ANGELO'S BABY BOMBSHELL	Janice Lynn
NEWBORN NEEDS A DAD	Dianne Drake
HIS MOTHERLESS LITTLE TWINS	Dianne Drake
WEDDING BELLS FOR THE VILLAGE NURSE	Abigail Gordon
HER LONG-LOST HUSBAND	Josie Metcalfe

MILLS & BOON®